DARRYL

JACKIE ESS

CL◄SH

Copyright © 2021 by Jackie Ess

ISBN: 978-1-944866-84-6

Cover by Matthew Revert

CLASH Books

clashbooks.com

Troy, NY

Is there even one other like me — distracted —
his friend, his lover, lost to him?

Is he too as I am now ? Does he still rise in the morning, dejected, thinking who is lost to him? and

at night, awaking, think who is lost ?
Does he too harbor his friendship silent and endless?

harbor his anguish and passion ?
Does some stray reminder, or the casual mention of a
name, bring the fit back upon him, taciturn and
deprest?

Does he see himself reflected in me ? In these hours,
does he see the face of his hours reflected ?

—Walt Whitman, "Calamus 9"

PART 1: WINTER

LEBRON

YOU LIVE VICARIOUSLY THROUGH CELEBRITIES, I LIVE VICARIOUSLY through the guys who fuck my wife. But sure, ok, I'm the weird one. Let me ask you this: do you watch sports at all? I could ask, "what's the point if you aren't the one playing?" but it isn't exactly a fair question.

I think a lot about LeBron James. I can imagine his NBA rings on the bedside table, next to Mindy's wedding ring and these little antique porcelain ashtrays that Mindy's mom gave us for our wedding. I'll bet he's got a great grip, and big hands that move decisively. A touch with no tickle, no trepidation, no contingency plan, just going to exactly the right place and going straight there. That's basketball. I'm sure he's all-around athletic, but for some reason I specifically imagine his hands, moving Mindy around. 6'8", God.

But look, I know as well as you do that that's just a fantasy. And even in fantasy I try to mostly keep this stuff confined to people confirmed to be in the lifestyle, which I'm pretty sure he isn't. Cause it's a little objectifying, you know? I try to do right by people. He's a professional athlete, he's focused on the game. Focused on, I don't know, his own family, probably. His own problems. Or maybe just his own fun. I'm just saying that he's got a life--that he isn't just there for me to look at. Just because a guy can fuck my wife doesn't mean he wants to. That was a hard lesson for me to learn, actually. But I'm glad I thought it through. Cause I really don't want to project too much on the guy. It's bad enough that everybody wants to compare him to Michael Jordan. By the way, I don't want to start an argument about this stuff, but I do think he's better, and you know what? Even if he isn't a better player, I like him better. Jordan always gave me the willies. All I'm saying is that I'd never write a fan letter asking him to come meet us after a game, like:

Dear LeBron,

I want to see your strong perfect hands gripping my wife, palming practically her entire body.
[...]
I want her to have your baby.

Love,
Darryl

I'd never write that. I'd write, "Sincerely,"

TABOR

Last Saturday I drove up to Portland with a plan to hike Mt. Tabor, but I didn't do it. It's one of those things you always say you're going to do, but in the moment you find you don't really want to. It's a tiny thing, barely deserves the name of a mountain and I like to climb it just for the joke of it, to imagine myself as a mountaineer—"because it was there!"

As a kid I always liked alpine adventure stories, not sure what that means. But everybody has a type, I had a cousin who loved that James Bond movie, Thunderball, where they fight the bad guys with harpoons underwater. Then when we were in high school he was a books guy, he grew a beard before anybody else and he claimed to have read Moby Dick. I tried to read it too but got lost. Sub-Sub-Sub-Sub-Librarian? All I know is it's all underwater. Maybe a submarine. Not for me, I had my head in the clouds.

I still remember an episode of "Get Smart" where the villain, who's Swiss, is identified by the instinctive slalom of his walk. I imagined a place where everywhere we walked it was always uphill or always down, practically vertical. The real Switzerland is nothing like that. I've been there once, as a teenager, mostly in Lausanne. There are mountains, but there are mountains here too. Europe is generally overrated that way, it's just more of here but more expensive. I think I'd have to get a job if I lived there. I don't see my inheritance as being enough to run with the Strasbourg set. Mainly I couldn't take the house with me. But I wonder if it's true that they're more enlightened about cuckolding in France? People are always saying that.

I didn't end up hiking Tabor but I drove out there for a few minutes. Figured why not take in a little nature with my coffee. I'm not really a nature guy, which is a shame, living out here. Everybody else is, but I think maybe they don't mean it, they're doing it because they're supposed to. One foot in front of the other until they're at the top of the hill. Then what? Walk back down?

I saw a guy at the top. That felt good. Just that somebody climbed it, that was enough. I waved to him, just a little hiker's salute, then wondered if he wouldn't think that was weird. But I probably looked like an ant to him, it doesn't matter. He probably wasn't even looking this way. Tabor is actually even smaller than the hills around Eugene, it's just funny to me that it's right in a city like that. It's the opposite of nature, and so weak. Apparently it used to be a volcano. Maybe he was going to throw himself in like that Greek guy, Empedocles? Don't worry, it's dormant.

GROSS

SOMETHING I WAS THINKING ABOUT—IF YOU'D NEVER HEARD OF sex it would sound pretty fucked up, right? You'd probably wonder if it was safe. Maybe you'd think it was gross. But somehow we mostly all come around. And we figure out how to do it, at least passably. Is that the species at work in us? It's surprising that there isn't more of a range of responses. Everybody wants to stick it in. Except me, I want to watch a guy stick it in. So here I am watching Bill fuck my wife. I can't do it like Bill, not any more than I can play like LeBron, but I did what I could and it was alright for a while, before we really knew what was possible. That's what's different about me, maybe. I want to know.

In most ways, though, I follow the pack. I put a lot of stock in what's "normal" in my life. So it was easy to assume I was done growing up when I grew up. I can fuck—sort of, drink coffee—with milk, whisky—with soda, beer, grow a beard (well, that might be a stretch). I could join the army! It's not like I did all that, but what I'm saying is, they're all acquired tastes. Imagine saying to a kid "not only are you gonna like this, but your life, your whole world, is going to revolve around it. You're going to take pride in taking it as bitter as you can." About coffee, war, fucking. It's hard to believe. I would have pushed back. I think that's why teenagers are the way they are, not that mine was.

I had to work through all of these aversions to everything bitter, gross, scary, and jealousy is kind of the same way, kind of belongs on that list. Finding out about Mindy and Bill for the first time hurt intensely, even as deep down I knew, I'd been setting this up and wanting it to happen for months. We talked about that, and Mindy told me about the cuckolding lifestyle. I spent some time online, I don't know, that was September. We're starting to get the hang of it.

Sometimes I feel like my heart is a long hallway with every door locked. Locked by "gross," "humiliating," "unsafe," "bitter," or just in chastity. Exploring this lifestyle feels like unlocking those doors one at a time, except I guess for the last one.

This must sound touchy-feely. It's certainly not at all how I was raised to be. But isn't that the problem? Everything they told me to be, I never could be. I never could be because I never was. Does that make sense? And even if you're just like me, even if I try to show you, you won't see me. Not for years. I feel like the Invisible Man. Actually I've never seen that movie or read the book (are they even related? I'm remembering someone taped up like a mummy, but I think the book was about a black guy?). I should see if it's on Netflix and stop talking into the void. I need to think about it more when I'm sober. I can't even relate to what I just wrote. Or maybe I'm just scared because I know what it means. Lonely road for us, ain't it?

Maybe I should lay off the G. Mindy doesn't like me taking it and I think she's right, but I feel like I've been having these breakthroughs. I get very emotionally clear. I was never a drug guy but this stuff levels me out. I buy it direct from a chemist in Taiwan and just take it solo. I think it might be helping me to lose weight, cause it's got less calories than beer, but here's the main thing: it isn't bitter! Besides, I'm safe with it, I always dye it the same color of blue, I never mix it with alcohol, I measure my dose with a syringe, and I keep it sealed to prevent evaporation. I've always been a fastidious guy. The one thing I do that's different I guess is drop in a packet of nutrasweet. Mmm.

Sunday morning, Bill let me touch it. That was interesting. He asked if I wanted to and I didn't know what to say. I'd never put my hands on another guy like that before. So that's what a real man feels like. Different for sure. I guess until that moment I thought "hard" was a metaphor. I thought it would be warmer, in a way. I wanted to maybe do something with it but I didn't, I wasn't sure how he'd react, so I just palmed it for a second and gave him a quick stroke. Actually, I didn't know what to do, I just wanted something to happen, but nothing did. They just shooed me away as usual and I made the coffee.

NEW YEAR

I WAS GONNA POST MY NEW YEAR'S RESOLUTIONS BUT I DON'T know what to say. I've got some issues and I need to work on them. On New Years Eve I asked Bill to do something for me, something that was too far. I don't remember saying it. But I remember him shaking his head, walking out. He had a friend who died in a similar situation a few years ago. How could I have known? He hasn't called back.

I can't even face Mindy. "Sorry I ruined everybody's night by asking your boyfriend to murder me." "Sorry I had so much to drink." "No I wasn't drinking exactly but I've been buying drugs on the internet again." "I think I might need help." As I say I don't remember but if I ever said anything like that it was definitely a joke. I'm not suicidal. I'm here for the whole ride. Still. Fucked up. "In vino veritas" type of situation. If I really said it, then I know that shit is in my head somewhere. And even if I don't remember it, they do.

So I fucked up. But I can't remember. It puts you in a reflective mood, for sure. I've sometimes been surprised by that, thinking about times Mindy told me I was laughing in my sleep, or crying, or seemed afraid. And I could never remember my dreams when she asked, often I do, but whenever she asked me it was never there.

I went for a walk down by the Willamette and thought a lot

about what connects my life to life, the old protein machine from soup to present. Maybe what I like so much about being in nature sometimes is seeing this level where it's all automatic. Does that make any sense? It's confirming and it's relaxing. There's a feeling of being left behind by all of it. By people too. It's intense, humiliating, and kind of numb. I think I must not be wired right. Well, I know that.

Bill and Mindy don't really need me, right? That's the joke. But the other puzzle is this. Why can't I seem to move past this moment where everything is revealed, confirmed, the precise moment when we break the connection? The door, which was open a crack, closing. The rotary dial phone, clattering to the floor. My wife, lost to the brute. And I'm lost too, in this kind of ecstasy of shame that takes me out of myself, and deeper into this kind of ocean roar feeling.

I don't think Bill or Mindy see things the way I do, they just see me as some kind of weird voyeur. Fetish guy. For them it's just a way to feel good, to break the rules, to relax a little. I think it scares them, the way I feel about it. I feel everything too much. I wish I didn't feel anything at all sometimes. That's what the G helps with. Anxiety: gone.

Mindy said we can keep going on the conditions that Bill doesn't have to deal with me and that I go to therapy. I'm gonna do that for now, but I sure hope I get to see more of Bill when things cool off. Imagine that, Darryl Cook, normal guy! Fuck it, make me like the rest of them. I can't deal with this anymore.

I'm not used to talking about my feelings with people, it comes out weird. They get scared, which makes me feel like more of a freak. Thanks. Maybe in therapy that won't happen.

TRIGGER

I DON'T EVEN KNOW WHAT TIME IT HAPPENS ANYMORE, OR WHAT they talk about. Is Mindy going to leave me? I think I would if I were her. It isn't hot in the same way if I'm stuck on the outside. Or maybe it is. It's happening and I guess that's enough. It isn't "hot" but it's still happening. That's enough.

I've been laying off the G. I wonder if that Taiwanese chemist is missing his best customer. I'll log on to make another order and he'll say "Darryl, so good to see you, been missing you, how's the wife?" I haven't tried to talk about my feelings without taking G for a long time, I'm realizing. It feels clear, intense, a little scary. Mostly I'm just tired all the time. I wish I had a friend. I wish I was a priest, or a woman, or nothing at all. Actually I don't wish any of that I just wish I didn't have to be what I am. How do you get motivated to make a change? Hypnosis?

Bill was I guess "triggered" by what I said when I was drunk. His friend from college had been kind of a fetish guy who died? Or was it his cousin? Or his brother? I actually didn't understand the story. I didn't see much in common between me and that guy but I didn't want to drag Bill over hard memories. He seemed to be about to cry. We've all lost people. It's easy to forget a big guy like that has a heart.

That's actually what kills me the most. When he was just a big brute sex machine it was easier to maintain a sense of relevance. That's the boyfriend, I'm the husband. He can fuck and I can talk. But he's a real person. He's sweet, he's actually sweeter than me. I think that must be the appeal of him for Mindy, he doesn't just get her off, he gets her. He doesn't just get to have a big hard cock, he gets to be a real person with real feelings, and real reasons for them. Thinking about that put me right back on my spiral of shame. Am I jealous of Bill's loss? I guess I'm jealous of anybody who cries at the right times. I'm crying too, but in my sleep, or because of a cuckolding fantasy that's all in my head, or now it's in my bedroom, or I got too high. I don't even feel real to myself.

I can't shake the feeling that she's going to leave me. She's going to leave me and I'm going to be alone. So that I'd be back to square one, just older now. I turned 11 last year. I always like to say that, cause I was born on a leap day and I only get a birthday every four years. It's more like I'm 45, I just don't have birthday parties.

I'm not going to turn the wheel one more time. I can't do it. No energy. I have to make it work. Working from right here, from this moment, could I make Mindy feel anything but contempt for me? For what I am? It's the old hero's journey, I suppose. Well, I've got pluck, more pluck than anybody. I'm living proof of that, I'm alive.

I think I'll march home right now and tell Mindy that. I'll win her back. We'll look back and laugh. She told me to stay out all day but this is too important, I can't lose the moment. If Bill's there, I'll just leave.

SNEAK

BILL AND MINDY WERE SO QUIET THAT I THOUGHT THEY WEREN'T at the house, that they must have gone out. They thought I'd been sneaking around listening to them. And I really wasn't! But I can see how they'd think that, I wouldn't believe me. I don't know if I believe me right now. Typical Darryl misunderstanding, I guess. We did manage to talk a little.

I think my basic miscalculation in all of this was thinking that Mindy was into the lifestyle. She's not. She always had a boyfriend, or a husband, or as I found out eventually, both. But she doesn't want to play with jealousy or pain. She just thought it was fun to break the rules. She wants what she wants. I want what I don't want, or something. Is everybody else simpler than me or is that just the view from the inside?

She had divorce papers printed out. No-fault. I actually know something about that, the laws are different from state to state and Oregon is a very easy place to get divorced if you don't have any money or property. But we've got both, so we couldn't do this thing without lawyers even if we wanted to. And I don't want to. I need another chance. I can't ask for chances right now so I asked her to give me time. Supposedly Bill might move in, he lost his job recently. I said it might be better just to help him with the bills at his current place. Everybody liked that, but she told me to stay with my aunt Farol out in Coburg anyway. What the hell am I supposed to tell her?

This doesn't feel as good as I imagined. I remember this feeling from the first time I got my heart broken, in college. Greg. He was my roommate. I remember how my girlfriend had never had an orgasm, and there I was in the top bunk pretending not to be there as he took her over the edge again and again and wishing that I would, sir, die. Just like now, when she left me I flailed and made all kinds of suggestions. It was too late. I'm just out of it. I don't matter anymore.

I need some G.

HOSPITAL

MINDY SIGNED TO GET ME OUT OF THE HOSPITAL THIS MORNING. I think I was there for three days but it felt like time out of time. First I was in the regular hospital, I don't remember that, then I was at a mental facility. It feels like I was there forever. I think a lot of stuff is going to change. I'm not going to do anything in the lifestyle for a while. I didn't want to tell them about that because I thought they'd lock me up forever if they knew. Better to play "depressed." I have those problems. Nobody believes me but I wasn't trying to kill myself, I was just reckless. It was stupid but it wasn't worse than stupid. Everybody thinks I tried to commit suicide and now it feels like I can't have a real conversation with any of them. They all look so worried about me, and if I tell them what happened they just think I'm spinning rationalizations. I get it. I caught a glimpse of myself in the mirror and thought, "you look like a guy that's seen some shit." Guess I have. Just wish I could remember it. Maybe it's better that I can't.

I wish I knew how to talk about what it was like in the hospital or about the people I met there. Though maybe they'd like their privacy. People have got some serious problems. I'm actually ok, I just take too much GHB. I guess it's not a very common drug anymore but it's the only one that ever really worked for me consistently. Funny to say it that way, cause I guess it doesn't really work for me if I'm overdosing by the river. But I was having a hard day? People do make mistakes. A lot of people around here are into methamphetamines, which just seems grimy to me. I don't even really like to drink.

CLIVE

QUICK UPDATE FROM ME. I'M STILL LIVING THE LIFE, STARTED therapy, patching stuff up with Bill, but cautiously. "Wife comes at you fast." I said that to him and he laughed, he's such a great guy.

My new therapist smiled at me in a strange way when I said her name. I asked if he knew her and he mumbled something about confidentiality. I mean, Mindy's name. He asked me a lot of distracting questions about my mother and whether Mindy was on the pill. What the hell are these headshrinkers trying to do? I think following through on the therapy is going to be a good thing anyway. It's Freud, man. They make everything about sex and babies. "Yeah, a nuvaring now, why?" No answer. Just more scribbling in that damn notebook.

We're going to try couples therapy with this guy. It bugs me that his name is Clive. That's not fair, but I guess he's British or something. Definitely foreign. I do think it works though. When I got home from therapy, I flushed the last of my G. That seems like a huge thing and I didn't know how to say it. I could just buy more online, but I know I'm not going to. I'm on the straight and narrow now. I wish I could get out of all this therapy, but I've got to admit, I don't know where I got the resolve. So maybe from Clive, maybe it works. Why does he want to do the therapy sessions at our house?

BRITISH

Couples therapy was really weird. It felt like Clive and Mindy were having a conversation I wasn't in on. He weirdly suggested that he'd like to watch me and Mindy have sex. He's kind of an alternative guy, "somatic" was the word he used. It was hard for me. He made eye contact with Mindy the whole time, scribbled in his notebook and left. Is he even a real therapist?

I guess I saw the diploma and Mindy says insurance is paying for it. She handles the money, I don't know. But still, how embarrassing. I don't see how it really fixes any of my problems. Maybe it doesn't have to, it's a "helping relationship," that's enough. Before leaving, he gave us both massages, which I thought was a nice touch. Really strong hands. Is this how they do things in Merry Olde England? I keep forgetting to ask where he's from.

Mindy seemed to think he was great, so we'll do another session. But there's a moment I can't get out of my head from when we were having sex. Just as I was about to cum, Clive looked up from his notebook and shook his head at me. Like I was doing something I shouldn't be doing. What the hell? I'm not that bad at this. Why would he do that? I thought the whole point of therapists was to be non-judgmental. I read Carl Rogers in college, I remember this stuff.

Therapy shouldn't be a British guy who looks like my dad making fun of how I have sex. Frankly I'm a little bit steamed, even though it's similar in a way to the cuckolding scenes we've done before. And now apparently in spite of the sober thing he wants to give us some drug that makes us more open-hearted. That'll be the third session.

PSYCHOSOMATIC ADDICT INSANE

We had our second session with Clive today. I guess he likes to work very intensely with clients, a lot of sessions in a row. I brought up my concerns about the head-shaking. He didn't say anything in response, just looked at me for a long time and I became aware that his eyes are very gray. I've actually never seen eyes like that. We told him more about Bill and he said we would try some forms of aversion therapy and hypnosis, he asked me not to look anything up online. I guess there's a problem of people talking themselves out of this stuff, or into it, psychosomatic.

He's going to give us this drug, I think it's the same as ecstasy. A pharmaceutical version of it. I once did try ecstasy at a party in the nineties, without really knowing what it was. I hugged a lot of people. I danced to music that I thought was crap but was perfect at the time. But I'm not supposed to think about it as drugs, we're getting in touch with our feelings. That's what it's about. In the end I don't think any of the drugs ever worked for me except G, because all I really want is to check out. It makes me reflective, which I haven't heard anybody else talk about, but maybe it's just that it lets me out of wherever I'm stuck. Maybe when I'm sober I'm too anxious to think.

HARMONY

I DON'T KNOW WHAT TO SAY, I'M STILL FLYING OR SOMETHING. THE rush is amazing and I feel like I had to write something down and they're busy. I have to remember this feeling. What even happened? Clive laid out three pills of MDMA and gestured for me to take one. I gulped it down dry and he smiled and put the other two away. "You and Mindy aren't taking any?"

"We won't need it."

Then we sat in silence for about fifteen minutes. I started to feel this kind of, I don't know how to describe it. I was clawing at the couch trying to feel more of the texture, it was nothing psychological. There are no psychological blocks at all. I can talk about anything and all I want to do is feel. I can feel everything. I can't remember, but I can feel, and everything feels gentle and open.

And Clive, those beautiful gray eyes, I think they could see into your soul if you let them. He turned to Mindy and said "would you like to have an orgasm?" It was a funny question, so direct and not even exactly sexual. She nodded, silently, as if hypnotized, which actually I wonder if she was. I don't think she was or that I am. She nodded and he stared, and then he asked, "do you want Darryl in the room?"

"Is it safe for him in this condition?" Mindy cares about me so much.

"First tell me what you want."

Clive has a funny way of controlling the conversation and also a kind of funny way of talking about sex. He told Mindy to take a shower and come back into the room ready, then turned to me. "Is it working, Darryl?"

I felt very harmonious in my body and in what was about to happen. Clive the British psychologist who definitely isn't British was going to fuck my wife in front of me. He's doing this thing for me, and he's doing it for a reason. It's actually a beautiful thing, and way down in the heart I felt something. A stirring of what I think is called "compersion." I read about that on a poly website once. Those people are so magical, like I think they're really deluded, open relationships hurt more than they know how to admit. But they love each other in spite of the pain. I think they all know that, and I started to cry at the seriousness of what they were taking on, how unmoored they are from a normal life. I am too, but we don't know how to talk to each other. I'm a cuck, that's not enlightened, I'm doing this the old way. But maybe we can untie the knot, maybe we can get it together.

Usually I'd be thinking about how pathetic I am, how come I can't be like Clive, how come I can't be like Bill, how come I can't be like Mindy. Lord knows I can't be. I noticed that he'd been hard for our whole conversation, it seemed so natural that I wondered if he wasn't just always. But that isn't possible. I think that would be called priapism, it's a dangerous condition. I said I wanted to lie down on the floor, to melt. He said "let yourself" and turned on some music which I recognized as dub or something like it. I asked who it was.

"Simon Posford."

"This is really cool."

"Simon's a friend, actually."

Of course Clive would know everyone. I don't even care if he's lying, the music is magical. He retrieved several crystals from his briefcase and Mindy returned in a towel. Clive simply stared into space again, not needing to say anything. She handed me the towel and lay down silently on the chaise longue, a really wonderful piece of furniture from my aunt

Farol. She always had so much style, she doesn't belong here. I don't think she wanted me to belong here either, thinking back to that summer in Lausanne, the French lessons. But I do, I always felt like I disappointed the family by being such a regular guy. I'd never buy something like that, but now I see why she would. Maybe I would. It's perfect what with Clive being a psychologist. And so much more than that. Then he did his magic. Do I need to go into detail? Emotionally what was going on here was so much purer and more beautiful than just sex.

Normally I think "why do we need that?" or like the other day "what links my life to life?" I normally need this grinding, punishing confirmation of that feeling. But this time everything was kind. The words that kept running through my mind were "we can forgive ourselves for needing this, for needing to get fucked this way." Actually, I wondered if I couldn't too, get fucked I mean. I didn't ask Clive, I just did my best spiritual bow and left the room.

I'm in the bedroom now and it's starting to wear off. They're still going. I'm glad I wrote all this down because it's so hard to remember already. I want to sleep for a year or maybe bump it up with another pill, but I can't interrupt. Why is it so short? And maybe I need to think about some stuff and not write. Thank you so much, Clive. I don't understand what you've done to us but maybe I don't need to. Something struck me about Clive: I think he must be very alone, what does it mean that he hides?

It's funny to imagine what he must mean when he says "Simon is a friend." I could believe it, he has the air of being well-traveled, but I feel like it's more likely that he went to some parties and Simon was the DJ, and they talked a bit. Would Simon say Clive is a friend or even remember him? Probably not, right? It seems sad that Clive has to lie about who his friends are. How can a guy like that even have friends? Maybe by taking a lot of this stuff.

THE HANGOVER 1

THIS MORNING I FELT DOWN, USED UP, FLAT. EVERYTHING IS FINE but very gray. The northwest weather doesn't help. I always think people in other parts of the country must celebrate Valentine's day differently, it might be cold but at least you can see the sun. Deep February in Eugene is just this dead gray that feels like forever. I don't even get a birthday, most years. I took a vitamin D supplement, then another. Does it even do anything? I'm scared of vitamin deficiency but I'm also scared of unregulated supplements. I don't know why I have that anxiety, Clive hands me a pill and I pop it in my mouth, not to mention, I was buying GHB from shady Taiwanese chemists for years. But somehow the vitamins bug me. Maybe I should tan, I'm tired of being so pasty white.

Mindy surprised me by saying that Clive would come back in the evening.

"It's not another session, don't worry about it."

"But—"

"It's none of your business, stay out of it."

I don't care how they fuck. Clive is silent, always in control. I'm just a little annoyed to be kicked out of my own bed. I wonder if it's guys who are into control like that who become therapists. Clive has a lot in common with his patients, probably.

Maybe it's just because he's British, like Hannibal Lecter. Is Hannibal Lecter even British? Is Clive? Hannibal Lecter is fucking my wife. Ok. I hope he doesn't eat her. Or me. Just let me sleep, I don't know. I just know my legs hang off the chaise lounge enough that I can't sleep on it, so I'm laid out on the twin bed in the guest room. I'm going to feel like shit tomorrow and I felt like shit today, I needed a real night's sleep.

So congratulations, Clive. You fucked her good. What's the point? What's the point of any of this? I've seen her take half a dozen guys like you in a single night—well, once. That's the secret, actually. Men are interchangeable. At least they're interchangeable above a certain level. Beneath that level they're disposable, which is where I am. In the bin.

But Clive is different. The impassable coldness, silence. Almost evil. Did you know he's not even a real therapist? He's just a hypno dom with a day job. Mindy met him at yoga or something. He does have a PsyD and used to practice. But for the last few years it's been all yoga, martial arts, hypnosis, and BDSM "dark energy work." He probably sells drugs to these people, that's the secret of all of those hippie types, they're all on acid.

I opened the door just a crack to see what was so special, since Mindy sounded like she was getting a workout and I saw quite a sight. How is that real? How is that physically possible?

Maybe Clive is a vampire. Where else could he find that much blood.

God, what if he gets her pregnant? What if I had to raise his child and the child was like him? Clive is a monster in two ways, it turns out. At least two. It's unsettling. I'm off to bed. 5-HTP and an orange, small glass of sherry. I'll be ok. I don't care. I don't care.

VAMPIRE

THIS IS A LONG SHOT, BUT I WAS THINKING ABOUT CLIVE. WHAT IF he was a, well, not a different species but a kind of human subtype. It might not have to be a type of person at all, just a rogue stretch of the genome, that had been brutally selected against. But instead of the gene dying out, it just raised the ante of sexual competition.

It could be something like a generalized mineral deficiency, so that they'd rarely reach adulthood. The gene's only hope of survival is to have its offspring raised by other mating pairs. That would require advanced and frightening strategies. Empathy would be a disadvantage here, but so would affectlessness. They'd have to fake it. So, no empathy, combined with profoundly high emotional intelligence devoted to simulating empathy, so as to blend with the ordinary human population.

The other thing they'd have to have is a huge dick. That's a mating strategy. And what about the mineral deficiency? Well, maybe this would come out as loving things like salty food, or blood. Could the myths and memories of vampires in our stories actually be a false understanding of a human subtype of huge-dicked psychopaths? Is that what Clive is? Except now he can take a multivitamin and live as long as the rest of us, barring my usual concerns about vitamins and supplements. He asked me if he could take some of mine and just tipped the bottle into his mouth, he must have eaten half the bottle. That's 50 pills. I've been thinking about that.

The monster, aged forty. The monster, with my wife. What are his intentions? Does a creature like that even have intentions? I read The Selfish Gene a few years ago and it really got to me, I think maybe this is what it was about. A lot of the guys on the cuckolding forum I use talk about it. I wish I knew more about evolution in general.

Oh and here's another funny thing about Clive. He isn't British at all, he just went to International schools. He's Dutch, I guess a bit Indonesian, mixed. I'd have said he was a white guy, but he's mixed race. The more you know. He talked a lot about how he doesn't think Asians see him as really Asian, because he looks white, was raised in Europe and America, doesn't have any Asian friends. I thought to myself, "well, they might be right," but I didn't want to say that to him. Anyway his problem isn't that he doesn't have a race, it's that he doesn't have a soul. There's something about the way he talks, it isn't even the movie accent, which is apparently called "transatlantic," it just sounds old fashioned to me. I guess in this case it'd be "transpacific." It's something deeper: Clive doesn't have a voice. Does that make sense? It's the imitation of human speech. Do I see him as an alien because he doesn't have a race, caught between white and Asian? I don't think it's that, I'm not a racist. There's really something about him.

I know something about him but he knows everything about me. About us. This could be trouble.

MONSTER MASH

MINDY SAID THAT CLIVE TOLD HER TO GET OFF OF BIRTH CONTROL and she made me come over and take the nuvaring out. She doesn't wear her wedding band either these days, but she always keeps it by the bed where Clive can see it. I wonder if he knows what I'm thinking. He might. I can't let him get her pregnant. I won't. Or if he does, I'll say, "Mindy, get an abortion or I'll leave." I won't raise that man's children. She says I shouldn't worry, that apparently Clive is only interested in pregnancy when the cuck is unaware, that otherwise he suspects the guy will resent the child or refuse to raise it as his own or just or nail it to a tree like Oedipus. That's right. I hope that's right. I already raised a son, Tony, and I was never sure if he was mine. I guess I have a guess.

Mindy bubbled in with a basketful of lube samples, I guess she's committed to trying to take all of Clive tomorrow. Clive is apparently a strong believer in silicone-based lubes, which I didn't even know about. I guess that at least rules out him being a silicon-based life form. Vampire? Maybe. Gray alien? Definitely not. Is it even safe? I guess she gave birth to our son. Anything's possible. I found something interesting, speaking of birth. It was a used up oxytocin inhaler, just lying on the nightstand by Mindy's wedding ring. Clive is so clinical. I don't believe he would have left something like that out by accident. It's a message.

I wonder if Bill would be willing to talk to me about what's going on now, it feels out of control. There's a smell in the room and I don't like it. I thought it was some kind of British— Dutch? —cologne but Clive just smells that way. He's not human.

I love watching a guy fuck my wife. Nothing better. But a human. Not a robot. Not an evolutionary fragment. Not a vampire. Not Hannibal Lecter. Not a fucking space alien.

What if he kills us both? What would even stop him?

Mindy said he was arrested today, but that it's no big deal. We're going to pay his bail. I don't know what to think, I don't even know what he was arrested for.

DON GIOVANNI

I WANT TO SAY MORE ABOUT CLIVE'S SITUATION BUT HIS LAWYER said I should be circumspect. Road rage, and it sounds like the other guy doesn't want to press charges. It should go away. Derek (the lawyer) and Clive are going to come over for dinner tomorrow. Supposedly Clive is a great cook (of course he is) and Derek knows wine (of course he does).

I talked to Bill for a while for the first time since New Year, just happened to run into him at the store and we had a beer. He's a good guy. I guess he's actually trying to get more into the cuckolding lifestyle as an alpha. Glad we didn't turn him off. It makes sense, he's got the equipment and he's just plain good to work with. I think it works better because he's a white guy, the racism would make it hard otherwise. Like you wouldn't believe how people talk on some of these websites. Even calling the guys "bulls" is probably fucked up. But I can't change everything. "Black bulls." I don't know. Is all of this happening because of slavery? Sometimes I think that about sports too. I guess Jason Williams is the exception that proves the rule, that was a white guy who could play basketball. But didn't they call him "white chocolate?"

I told Bill that if there was a Yelp for alphas, I'd give him five stars. He smiled and his smile was so genuine. Maybe it's just because of Clive, but I'm feeling starved for any kind of humanity at all. I told him it'd mean a lot if he came around and reminded Mindy, and he made a suggestion of his own.

He said I could come along and assist him on one of his bull errands soon. He's apparently been fucking the pastor's wife for a few years and she finally told him. Apparently it goes along with his alpha persona to have a servant, to be sort of the Leporello to his Don Giovanni, if you know opera at all. Actually Bill is a good guy and I think Don Giovanni wasn't. What the hell is that opera about? Don Giovanni always struck me as a creep, and I always wondered what it meant that a guy like that could be the hero of the story and we'd all just go along like it's nothing. It's the same way with Clint Eastwood. There's something fucked up going on and it's related to being a man, it's not just about opera. But anyway, Bill doesn't know about opera and I gave up trying to catch him up, actually I found myself hating the story more than I remembered as I started to describe it to him. Why do we do this to ourselves? What are men doing to women? It feels gross. Am I a feminist? I don't think I can be, but I'm an ally. Clive probably knows about opera. Clive knows everything.

Bill hugged me hard and said he had to go so I paid for our beers and walked home in a daze, for a moment just loving my life. It was like the squeeze of him stayed in me. I zoned out and forgot all about Clive, which felt better. And when I got home, I told Mindy I was getting straight into the shower and took a long hot one. When the water hits my neck, it's like I don't exist. How long was I in there? I felt feminine, almost. Very neutral and beautiful and clean. Like somehow Bill had loosened up a layer of dirt on me that was Don Juan and Clint Eastwood and everything else and now it comes right off under the water. What would it be like to be clean?

ETERNAL CHAMPION

I'VE BECOME SUCH A SPORTS GUY, ALL FROM A STUPID SEXUAL fantasy, and from trying to impress Bill. But I'm genuinely excited to see the Cavs play the Warriors tomorrow. It feels like a symbolically important game. I mean you've got LeBron, I sort of see him as the last hope of human beings. If you look at the Warriors, they're playing moneyball. They've turned basketball into golf, all the shots are from the other side of the court. There's no confrontation, no humanity. Just skill. Just San Francisco slickness. If you don't root for LeBron against that, are you even alive? I can't believe I'm saying all this, like am I a real sports guy now? I wonder if Bill would watch the game with me. I kinda wish Bill was my dad, or that my dad had been more like Bill, everything would have been a lot simpler that way. Instead he's my bull. I guess that works.

Full of dread about dinner with Clive later. I said that to Mindy and she said that she didn't care and threw up the horns. Wow. Is she becoming like him? I pray that Bill can bring her back to her senses and I sort of feel he's the only one who can. I imagine him as something like the hero with a thousand faces, the eternal champion. Oh Bill, my chevalier! And I, your squire! Though the storm rages and the road is long, you will defeat Clive and fuck my wife. Beautifully, honestly, good-hearted, and hard. Even now, thunderheads gather on the far horizon. Let me oil your armor, gather wild roots for your steed as we begin the perilous journey.

TOOTH AND CLAW

WHEN CLIVE ARRIVED HE IMMEDIATELY SET TO ROASTING FOUR Cornish game hens for dinner. I'd never eaten that before, but they're just single-serving chickens. I wonder how it must feel like to be that. Maybe I'm a single-serving man. Lord knows I'm not a cock. Fantastic balance of spices, but why was mine well done? Everyone else's was practically raw. I asked him. He just smiled in his usual inscrutable way. "Do you really like it that way, Darryl? Nature red in tooth and claw?" I think I've never been so afraid. He knows how to bring fear into the room just perfectly focused on me while saying something sort of innocuous, everybody else laughed. He added, "that's from Tennyson, 'In Memoriam'" and sort of chuckled and everyone acted like they knew what he meant and that it was something very sophisticated. But that was a threat!

Derek's eyes are the same as Clive's and he doesn't say anything. It scares the hell out of me. Through dinner, they wouldn't even acknowledge me, they keep saying things like, "your—" long pause, "husband," to Mindy. Over and over in a conversation that moved very fast, so that I can't understand anything except the insults, or sometimes just that I'm being insulted. These guys remind me of the cenobites from Hellraiser. I might have to take a walk. Not to mention, they brought coke. That really grinds my gears. I'm never going to get that bail money back, am I? First the hospital stay, then Clive's bail, I can only draw so much at a time from my inheritance. Derek cut three lines and handed me a large capsule of some white powder. He told me to go into the other room and take it, to lay out on the guest bed and wait for it to kick in. It was the first time he'd addressed me, and he seemed almost not to see me.

So I'm here now, in what used to be my son Tony's bedroom, before he went away to college, just staring at the pill. It could be cyanide for all I know. These guys are capable of anything. I don't think I have any choice but to take it. I'm not going to jump out the window. Maybe I'll die. I wish Bill were here. Fuck.

And what are they going to do to Mindy? She acts like she belongs to Clive now. And who are these guys? WHAT are they? Well, down the hatch. Screaming from the other room. Down the hatch. Can't think about it. Not fighting.

Fifteen minutes in I feel very peaceful, and the beginning of something, something, a kind of buzzing. It's such a sweetness. The light! The light!

THE HANGOVER 2

WHAT A DAY. I DON'T EVEN MIND THAT THE WARRIORS BEAT THE Cavs. Mindy's taking a nap, I feel light and alive and new. I'm just here with Bill, hanging out, absolutely present. I'm not drinking any beer but Bill's had a few. He let me do something for him and it was cool. I've never done that before. But I think I might need to chew more gum or something. Do I have a small jaw? He liked it. That's what counts.

We're going to run a little errand tomorrow night. Pastor Mark's wife talked him into trying out the lifestyle, sounds similar to how it was with my marriage. So they're into it. Is the whole damn city of Eugene? Meanwhile, Derek and Clive seem to have skipped town. So there goes the bail, which was a lot of my inheritance. I should check the bank statements. I just want more of those pills. 4-HO-DIPT was what they said it was in the morning. Like mushrooms, I think, in some chemical way. They said they'd sell me some more and that I should read a book about this stuff by a chemist who synthesized everything under the sun and fed it to all his friends. Interesting life, I think I will try to find the book. Maybe my old chemist has it, but I'm kind of scared to go back to the site, I don't know if I trust myself to stay away from G. Anyway, we're going to take Lisa, Mark's wife, on a date later, to a hotel bar in Portland. The plan is for me to pretend to be the Uber driver. Well, maybe that's creepy. I think it is. I'll ask Bill what he thinks.

And then it happened. God, the way Bill looked Lisa in the eye and said "my assistant stays in the room." This is what I've always wanted. And there I am, waiting with the towels. I think the best moment was when Pastor Mark walked in and shook his head.

"Lisa, we're going to Hell for this."

It's funny, that's where I just came from. Tryptamine ceno-bite nightmares of Derek and Clive. Gimp processions in the dungeon of infinity. Leather. Planets of ice. Was that heaven or hell? I might have to start going to church. But for now I think I'm ok.

It's hard to remember how gloomy I was just a month ago when I went down to the river, when I asked Bill to kill me. I can remember it now. It feels so stupid that I ever wanted to die. And now it's just me and Bill letting the good times roll. New Orleans style. Maybe every guy like me just needs a best friend with a big cock. That's how we feel alive. I almost begin to think we could solve all the world's problems.

It occurs to me, I haven't talked to Mindy very much about how things have been going for me. She seemed ok this morning. But her eyes were still different and I think I'm just not going to bother her for a few days.

Politics have been really stressing me out, and Mindy too. But Bill came over and sorted us out. Maybe everything's going to be ok. But supposedly Clive voted for this guy, it's disgusting. I don't want to get political but that fucking figures, man. What can you do? I'll just keep my head down for a few years, now that I've got something to do with it.

Bill for president!

JESUS

Pastor Mark wasn't as cool with all of this as we thought, so we decided to take a little road trip to Reno. Sometimes you have to let things cool off. Just let the dust settle a little and try to see some sunlight. Just me, Mindy, and Bill. We met a kind of remarkable person in Reno, a transwoman (I think that's the word now) named Oothoon. What a weird chick, man, but I get it. I get it now, the trans thing I mean. Bill was really into her, which surprised me, it ended up being Mindy who took the most convincing. But you can guess what happened.

The whole time I was distracted, thinking about what people like that must go through. Can you imagine being like that in high school? Just unreal, fucking awful. I wanted to ask but didn't. Maybe she was just a regular guy in high school. Maybe we had something in common there. But it's not the kind of thing you bring up. "Hi, could we talk about your painful memories?" We just partied, so much for sobriety. I've got to admit I had a few. Lillet and vodka. Bill had a few of those too, which surprised me, I think I'm always making him out to be "manly." He's all man, alright, but I guess "comfortable with his masculinity." I'm comfortable with his masculinity too. Feeling giddy just thinking about it. Then Oothoon surprised me even more, cheap beer and shots of Jack. I wonder if there's any of that kind closer to me, I mean, transwomen, not drunks. I mean, I don't know if she's a drunk. She's a poet though. And she can drink a lot. And she wears a denim jacket and has tattoos and bangs. Probably a drunk. Either way, I wish I had a friend like that. I hope Bill got her number. Not that any of us will pass through there again any time soon, I just like the idea that I'd see her again in a decade, in a different world.

Something I didn't get until I saw it: she actually had a dick and could probably fuck with it if she wanted to but it just wasn't what she was about. To be honest, I feel the same way. Like maybe I was built to take it, just built wrong. I'm not sure it even is wrong, it's just whatever it is. But I'm not gay, let alone trans. That's like next level gay. I'm just a beta, as Mindy's always reminding me. She likes that more, and so does Bill, I think. They don't like queers, except as an occasional one-off. That's dessert for them, not the main course. Bill is cooler with it, I think, though I can't figure out his attitude. I think I always expect him to be meaner about it because he's poor. But he's not stupid, he's not cruel. He's just straight. I wonder if Bill has any gay friends? I guess I wouldn't be surprised if he does. And gay isn't any weirder than whatever I am, right?

But ok, one honest question about the transgender: how come they all have such weird exotic names? If I was going to transition I'd just blend in, I'd be a Karen. The one we met took her name from a poem, she said, from William Blake. I don't remember. I can't get into poetry. Except maybe Sylvia Plath, but we all had that phase, right? Oothoon. Can you imagine having to repeat that name to people and sound it out a hundred times. Oothoon. It doesn't even have a gender! But I guess all of our names are like that if you go back far enough. What's Darryl? A small town in France? What's Adam or Jacob? The Bible? I don't know if that means I should read Visions of the Daughters of Albion or if it means I shouldn't bother. It's not like I know the Bible, though come to think of it maybe that's how I got into this mess. Still, I'm glad my name isn't a new one.

I don't know if it was the night we spent in Death Valley or what but this lifestyle feels less and less about me and Mindy. We're always gonna love each other, I know that. But my heart can't stay confined to that moment of truth, to the big reveal, to that feeling of confirming how it really is. And it is. It's all true! What Bill is, what I am, what that means. But eventually you can't just jerk off to that. You've got to follow through. What does following through look like? Am I supposed to kill myself? I don't want to. I never wanted to, even if everybody thinks I wanted to. What's a cuck to do?

What am I even saying? I don't know. That transwoman poet person really got under my skin. That was honest. I'm not like her either. I'm not like anybody. And I still get a charge from the scene of course, just seeing it happen. It's like Punch and Judy, the same characters forever. Newspaper cartoons. Coyote and roadrunner again and again, jumping off a cliff to slam my wife and accordion back. Tom and Jerry, but he gets the mouse, every time. Takes a bite. That's Clive. Or the Commedia Dell'Arte. I'm a little Pierrot and so adrift, cucked by Columbine. What the fuck does it all mean? How do you make a life out of that?

Like, here I am at 3AM, speeding through Tahoe National Forest while Bill lays into my wife across the back seat. And like, why? Why is my life about Bill and guys like him? I mean I like it, it's kind of relaxing. I never wanted to be the star of the show, I'm a simple guy, supporting cast, maybe.

What I got to thinking about is all those old Roman mystery cults and household gods, and how maybe I know the secret now. You meet one guy, one punishingly intense, serious cock, and you change your life for it. Even if you're a guy and can't get fucked by it. Or maybe you can, I don't know what that would feel like.

Maybe that's what humanity is, not the human species but humanity, culture, a sedimentation of little cults, each following one guy who's worth it. All that energy, all that history, somebody was packing heat. That's real religion: real dick. I think what scares Pastor Mark is that he knows that, he can't deny it now. Maybe that's what Jesus was, even. But he had to read it in his wife's eyes to know the truth. I did too. But when I saw it I didn't reject it. That's the difference between me and him. I believed my eyes. But aren't I a kind of doubting Thomas if I've got to watch the scene again and again? What would it take to convince me? What kind of Pentecost? It got me thinking about faith, what faith in this thing would mean, what would change.

There really is just one God. I don't know man, I got in touch with something when we were in the desert. That's what happens when you go out there. I brought some of those pills from Clive and we took them as we were driving back across Death Valley. Maybe I shouldn't have done that while I was driving but it was fine. Good to be back in Eugene again.

LITERARY

READING SOME OF MY OLD BOOKS FROM COLLEGE, MAKING QUOTES from them. "What does it matter how many lovers your wife has if none of them gives you the universe?" That's Jacques Lacan. More like La-cannot understand what the hell he's saying. I remember trying so hard with psychoanalysis, and finally feeling like it's all bullshit. I think the way they do, it's just that everything they say is wrong. Or who knows. Put on your best French accent and say «oui— et non.»

I can't wait until May, Oregon Winter is getting me down. I feel like I could do something productive with all this time indoors, like I could write a book on half-open relationships. Or read one, I wonder if anybody wrote one already. I'm not such a sophisticated guy but I feel like I've got some things to say. Maybe an online venue would publish it. Speaking of those, I found Oothoon, and sent her an email. I wonder if she'll write back. Another downside of having a stupid rare name is that if you have any kind of online profile at all people can always find you, but I'm happy for it this time.

Maybe I don't have to be sophisticated. One of my favorite things is when smart people aren't smart about everything. I don't get this so much with Mindy, we just talk about our lives. That's not to make her out to be dumb. She reads novels, much more than I do, she just never talks about them. She consumes them. Sex too. It's all yummy. Women are so good at that.

But that poet, she had something to say about everything. She had this huge theory about the Despicable Me franchise that I can't do justice. Minions, the little yellow cartoon monsters. Something about how much money they spent on marketing it. It was hard to believe they spent a billion dollars on that, or maybe it was a little less. Why? Seems like they sell themselves, kids love 'em. It made me wish I had more light-hearted stuff in my life, outside the bedroom. It's all heavy with me, without being serious. I love hiking but it's very meditative, in a heavy way. That's one mood, but I want to feel more alive, lighter. Maybe guys like me can't. That feeling of aliveness was always what I was interested in when I read about psychology. Who gets to feel alive? What makes us light up?

Maybe I should see a non-fake therapist. The Clive experience really messed that up for me but I don't want to give up. It's such a violation. But worth it, ultimately for the psychedelic intensity that he brought into the picture. I don't know, it feels like I'm just living between these intense trips. Some chemical, some fetish, some road, but it's got to be a trip. Nothing else feels real.

I hope she writes me back. I really need a friend I can rap with about this stuff, but it's so hard to start a conversation. All I'm saying is that I'd never write an email like,

Dear Oothoon,

I barely know you but I'm sure you can handle my problems and have the key to them. I don't think we're the same but I think you might be the only one in the world who can see the place I'm in now and can see me. I'm so lost. You took a different turn, one I can't understand, but I think it might be better. Rescue me from the puzzle of the dance.

Love,
Darryl

I'd never write that. I wrote, "Sincerely,

I don't know. I felt like I couldn't say any of that, but then I thought about how I'm always trying not to be a burden, maybe I act too cool. Hit send. At some point in my twenties I realized that a lot of people I meet get the impression that I don't like them. It's sad, who loves the world more than me? Whose submission to it is deeper? I just want to get drunk with you and talk about minions. Or I guess sober. With minions. I want to share moments like that moment in the desert when I forgot about my life and my problems and even myself. That's love and it's actually impersonal, indiscriminate.

I should go to bed, I've got to get up to cook breakfast for Bill and Mindy in a few hours. My wife and my best friend. My only friend, really. This is maybe out of nowhere but I'm glad I came back from the brink this Winter. I'm glad I'm here in whatever phase of life this is.

ANXIETY

JUDGE ME? COOL. HOW ABOUT NOT JUDGING ME INSTEAD. I MADE a passable Béarnaise this morning and I've gotten really good at poaching eggs. I was never into the brunch trend but I'm kind of glad it happened, it makes my kitchen skills more legible. I was always a breakfast guy and breakfast is a meal that's so essential, but it has no dignity in culinary circles. If I cooked cornish game hens like Clive you'd think I was a genius. But I cook eggs. Doesn't matter. This is the kind of husband I was born to be. For myself I usually just have yogurt, and if I'm lucky, well—

Mindy told me something interesting which is that for her the scenes we do aren't that interesting. It's just good sex. But the particular charge I'm getting from it just isn't there for her. That makes sense. She doesn't see the world in colors of male hierarchy and conflict. Even so, she mostly has a preference for the guys who come out on top. And who wouldn't? Not just for physical reasons, they're just more relaxed, confident. And man am I anything but. Or until recently that was true. I feel like I've been finding my way to a different kind of confidence, since the road trip.

Lately it feels not so much that I'm this weaker, lesser sort of man, but more like I'm not a man at all. I don't mean that in a trans way like Oothoon, just a different type of man. People won't stop talking about the trans thing lately, what's the deal

with that? I never actually met one until Oothoon, unless I
didn't know. But that's not what I mean, and anyway I'm talking
about me. I have a man's body (if you can call it that), and a
man's life. I'm a husband and a father. I picked up this burden
and I have to carry it all the way to the end. Even if the kid isn't
mine. Deep down I always knew that and Mindy eventually told
me. But you know what? He is. Love isn't just biology. I'm happy
to be his dad or whatever I am, and I'm glad in a way that the
curse ended with me. I've always been afraid that my unhappi-
ness was genetic. I just wish he'd call more.

Being gay would have been a lot simpler for sure. I feel like
I'm living proof that it's not a choice. I wonder if Bill would fuck
me just to see what it's like. One side of me thinks he wouldn't
care, a hole is a hole, another side thinks it'd ruin the friendship.
Maybe he's had sex with guys before? I think I won't bring it up.

I've been thinking a little more about how selfish this lifestyle is, in a way. There's no easy answers there and I think I
couldn't stop if I wanted to. But still, it's something to think
about. The thing is, when I see Bill really connect with it, really
pound it home, it's so intense. At that moment I don't care that
it's selfish and neither does he and neither does Mindy. We all
just remember what life is really about, the life that life really is.
It's like seeing a guy hit a hundred home runs at once. Even just
the sound of it, that's what does it for me. Even through the wall.

If that's what life's about, where do I fit into it? Again and
again, what links my life to life? The old cuckold's anxiety. But in
the moment? I could give a flying fuck. Instead I'll watch one.
Actually I prefer to listen.

Oh and Oothoon wrote back!

TRANS 101

HERE'S ONE THING I DON'T GET ABOUT THE TRANS THING. I'M INTO big dick and so is my wife. Are we still allowed to talk about it? Or is that too "Essentialist." College kids made that into a bad word at some point, but they never told me what was so wrong with it, I just know according to the smart gay people I'm not supposed to be it. Great, another way to be wrong.

I don't get a lot of the stuff in Oothoon's email, mostly I don't get why she's telling me. But it's very generous, she wrote back much more than I expected. I guess we've all got our issues. I mean, if I was trans I probably wouldn't be able to shut up about it either. Probably I'd be really cool about it but then when I got the chance to talk, I'd talk your ear off. But the long and short of it is that bodies don't matter but also that she has to change hers to be a woman. What? Isn't that a contradiction? And bodies do matter, they mean something. I believe in the trans thing because she looks like a chick. Because she is one. I believe in Bill because he's, well—I can't pretend I don't care about big dick, I do. Somehow Oothoon is a lot more annoying on the internet than she was in person but I think that's true of most people. But also I'd maybe better give this a little time to simmer, it's not like I know anything about it.

Thinking about that stuff too much seems like it could be a nightmare. Good thing it's not my problem, just a curiosity. And

even if I don't end up close friends with Oothoon I got some cool
book recommendations. If I could read for an hour a day, like,
imagine if I had been all this time. My life would be so different.
I'd be so wise. Best day to start is always today, I guess. It'll just
be nice not to be thinking about Bill's dick all the time, pulling
back just a millimeter from Mindy's cervix at the moment of
release. Furious pumping warmth. Or whatever's in there, actually I don't really think about the biological details so much, just
the pounding.

But why make it a project? She told me to read John Berryman, who I'd never even heard of. Whole worlds here that I
don't know about. Dream Songs.

LGBTC

CAN I JUST SAY HOW FUCKING WEIRD IT IS FOR ALL THESE PEOPLE to be talking about "cucks" as a political thing when you really are one? A gay friend on one of my message boards said that this is what he felt like when Eminem was breaking out in the nineties, everybody was saying "faggot" all the time. I can believe it. I'm sick of the slurs.

I don't see my political views as being connected to the guys who fuck my wife. I'm a pluralist. Clive's a Republican, or really kind of the extreme right wing fringe of that. Bill's a Democrat, and a union guy first. Reasonable people can disagree about this stuff, and they can do it in my bedroom.

I was going to say something like "never apologize for being a beta" but apologizing is kinda what we do. So that can't be the slogan. I don't see people like me as ever forming a pride identity like LGBT or whatever. LGBTC.

But that sucks in a way. There's probably a lot of people like me, we just don't want to shout it in the damn street. Is that self-hatred? No, I think it's just honesty, it reflects a difference of personality. We're never going to be out there beating a drum. The alphas though, they've got more to be proud of. Maybe they could carry the lifestyle. I keep thinking that they ought to have a union. But there's too many guys like Clive for that.

Whatever, like I said, I'm not a political guy. This is probably half-baked. But can you imagine if people started Identifying as Hung. I can't stop laughing. Probably Oothoon thinks you can do that.

I said to Oothoon that I thought we cuckolds are the only sexual orientation that's about the truth. Everybody else is about performance, pleasure, recognition. Is that why people seem to hate us so much lately? Maybe watching and listening are the bravest things a guy can do. Can you face your own inferiority? Can you watch yourself be replaced?

I'm ready for aging and I'm ready for the technological future. Are you? I think Clive isn't, he's holding onto a past that can never come back. All these guys are, and it's very weird, they see themselves as so strong but as victims at the same time. Why is that? Like we're all supposed to mourn a world that's no longer ruled by strong men. But it still is! And if they're so strong they ought to take it back themselves. It's all pity for the pitiless. Then they become fascists. I don't want to ask Clive about this stuff because I think he really might be a Nazi or something. The only reason I think he's not is because he's mixed. Could an Indonesian guy be a fascist? I should ask Clive what he knows about Suharto. Actually I think I won't.

LEADER OF THE PACK

I WISH I WAS CONSULTED SOMETIMES. THIS MORNING I WOKE UP TO the doorbell ringing and Mindy shouting at me from the bedroom. "Ok! The blindfold's on, you can send the first one in!" I knew absolutely nothing about these guys and I had to make smalltalk with them all day.

It was good in the end, they had cool stories. I guess some guy Mindy met on Craigslist got all of his buddies from the biker bar in Coburg. Well, that was the link. These motorcycle guys are amazing, I could never do it. I'd be terrified. Every corner. I think it goes without saying that they gave it to her good. One of the guys, Patrick, said he'd take me for a ride later. Patrick is cool, I wonder if Bill knows him.

Travails and follies of a cuck, I suppose. I had a particularly good conversation with Patrick, who's in an open marriage and apparently isn't always the aggressive one. That was the first time I'd met a guy in person who was in the lifestyle on my side. Though not exactly like I'm doing it. He's not a cuck, they just both have lovers. It seemed a little more sophisticated than what I'm doing but also a little hippy-dippy. "Compersion." He told me to read The Ethical Slut, and I suggested he read Marquis de Sade. He asked me "are you really so hardcore, Darryl? I've read some de Sade and put it down, he's mean." He's right. I just wanted to seem like I'd read something too. I don't want to live in de Sade's world. I should read some of Oothoon's recommendations. I might try to hang out with him again. Yet Another Effort, Oregonians, If You Would Become Alphas.

FREEDOM

I BELIEVE IN MERITOCRACY—IN THE BEDROOM. BUT SERIOUSLY, I don't see the relationship between the political things people say online and what I do in the bedroom or watch through a crack in the door or listen to with a glass to the wall.

I was thinking about what positive cuck representation would look like. I heard about the Bechdel test, but I don't think that would work for us. We're most ourselves as cucks when we're focused on others. There's not really any way around that. There can't really be a cuckold community. We're stuck on the edge of everybody else's. It sucks. I was talking about this yesterday with Oothoon, how we're not "queer."

I feel really lost sometimes. The insults don't help. I do have a sense of humor about this stuff, anybody who knows me knows that, and some of the jokes are funny. Actually before I was in the lifestyle I used to hang around 4chan and places like that with these young guys and laugh a little too hard at the jokes. I think there are a lot of guys like me on there, and a lot of guys like Clive. Some of them seem to know way too much about the lifestyle. From experience? Or just fixated?

I wish it was easier to talk about what it felt like. To be a dude who felt at odds but not yet ready to be a cuck. Or not even conscious, not knowing what it is or that it's you. I figure most of us weren't born knowing. God knows I wasn't. Another way it isn't like being gay. I wonder how many of those guys would be happier like me.

I don't think I can really advertise my point of view, since I wear it on my sleeve that I've got problems. But you know what? We all do. There's not a formula for happiness but I can't tell you how much better it is to be yourself. What would my life be like if I couldn't watch Mindy with guys like Bill, Patrick, the bikers, hell, even Clive.

Honesty is the best feeling ever, dude. Let the truth set you free!

YE SHALL KNOW THE TRUTH

I WENT TO THE LIBRARY THE OTHER DAY AND NOTICED AN engraving. "YE SHALL KNOW THE TRUTH." I already do.

Remember that show in the nineties where the joker guy played this dopey high school kid, Jordan Catalano I think? I wish I could have looked like that when we were younger. We did look alike. But my aesthetic was always a little more clean cut. I admire guys that can let their hair down a little. I never grew mine out. My dad would never have let me live it down. He's gone now, and I remember thinking when he passed that now I can be anyone, I can't disappoint him anymore. But I was already me, too late. His death opened a door that I no longer had the energy to walk through. I just wish I could tell him about my life, whatever the reaction. He wouldn't get it. But that was the last guy on this planet who really wanted me to do right. Mom cares but it isn't the same. She wants me to be ok. He wanted me to be upright. I think I'm neither. But I'm fighting for something now. That's new.

Even as everybody's talking about it now, the cuckolding life-style is still pretty stigmatized. We're not "out." I was talking to Oothoon about that. Like, you think of some of the old gay guys and you know they're all fucked up, there are just some pre-liberation attitudes. You know, the rich old fairies who'll say "I don't want another queen, honey, I need a man!" Silk scarf guys.

I've got to figure I'm a pre-liberation cuck. Makes me wonder what the next generation of cuckolds will think about me. Maybe it won't be nice. I guess by writing this down I'm taking a chance on finding out.

I saw a rainbow out the window today and was thinking about the pot of gold at the end of it. Mindy and Patrick didn't want to come look. The way I see it, I don't need the gold. My treasure is right here. I wonder if taking psychedelics helps me see that, maybe I should be doing that more often. Once per season? I'll ask Clive what he knows, it might be possible to do this stuff too much. I don't want to go crazy.

Clive should get a phone. Having a pager in 2017 is so weird, I can't deal with that level of criminality. I guess we're all "queer" in that way. But I just want to be a regular guy. I am a regular guy. Leaving a 3 for "she's ready, so come over and fuck my wife" and a 4 for "bring more of that stuff you brought last time." Things haven't changed much in 25 years.

I've been thinking about writing more. But being a writer seems like hell, I was talking to Oothoon about this. Why put so much time into stuff nobody reads? Why not just role-play the characters or something? She can't seem to publish anything and I keep asking why she cares about publication, just put it up online. She's on the computer 24/7 and so is anyone who'd ever read her book. She's not going to be Jodi Picoult anyway. But it's all a fantasy, it's a self-image thing, I think that's why she uses a typewriter.

Deep down I always wished I could be a writer too, I did have that dream a little. But we live in the modern world. I don't know. Mindy made fun of me for buying us a rotary dial phone, but I like hearing her talk to me on it when she's got a guy over, or even just panting. It's got a warmer sound. But my rotary dial telephone and my friend's typewriter are ultimately gonna suffer the same fate. We ought to get real, catch up to the times.

FROG'S EYE VIEW

TALKED A LITTLE WITH CLIVE ABOUT WHAT HE AND HIS FRIENDS have against us cucks. I'm starting to get it, although I don't agree. They have a very complete picture of the rejection or devaluation of a man. Physically, as a beta, sexually, as an incel, and economically as a NEET. Their resentment of cucks is that we recognize this abject situation and rationalize it or find pleasure in it. Our view of the world is similar, it's as though we've taken the red pill but it didn't make us want to fight back.

Obviously this is something that they fear in themselves, that after all they might have hold of the truth but it's checkmate anyway. The hatred of homosexuals works along similar lines but it's more complicated. The homosexual basically rejects Clive's worldview, he wants something else. Eventually you recognize that difference and there's less of a basis for conflict. We can imagine a gay right wing, and there even sort of is one.

But Clive and I, we know the same truth and have to contend forever over what it means. Our fates are bound up together, and not only because he's my therapist and my dealer and I paid his bail and he fucks my wife and I love it. We share a vision.

I think the right wing obsession with cucks and other forms of failed masculinity will outlive the homophobia that used to be their game. But in my opinion, and this may be the optimism of the morning's first sip of coffee, the cucks will win. We take the hierarchy of guys more seriously, in a sense, than the frogmen.

See, what's puzzling about their point of view, and here I'm not talking about big-dicked psychopaths like Clive, but the rest. They believe in a hierarchy, see themselves near the bottom, so far we agree and I'm there too. But they think they can reverse it by thinking. By reading forums. By taking a red pill. Eat a handful, buddy, nothing's gonna change. We both know what this world is like. Good luck! Oothoon's pills work. Clive's pills work. Is the red pill gonna add an inch? Maybe. But here's the thing about an inch: it's not two inches. So Bill's got you beat, and so does LeBron.

I wish I could be like some of you guys, really, I do. But all I can be is myself. Hopelessly, despicably, me. Minion style. The one and only Darryl Cook, or Darryl Cuck.

ACTING

MINDY JUST GAVE ME A TOY OSCAR AND SAID I WAS THE BEST supporting actor in our marriage. Bill's playing the lead. What a lovely, thoughtful gift! Meanwhile, Clive jokingly diagnosed me as having a "cluster beta" personality disorder. It was a mean joke but it got me reading some stuff online. I was going to say my problems aren't so severe, but come to think of it, I was hospitalized only a month or two ago. We're in the longest part of Winter. It's possible.

Am I borderline? I don't really want a diagnosis. Once I got stabilized I got the hell out of the hospital. I checked out against medical advice, which has turned out to be hell on my finances because it meant insurance didn't pay. But this stuff is compelling, feels familiar. But unlike these borderlines, I feel like I have an ok way of dealing with my problems. I bet a lot of people who get this diagnosis are really repressed cucks or something. That's a pretty big "or something," though.

So many different kinds of people in the world! I'm glad to have a friend that's a therapist, and who's easygoing about professional, sexual, and matrimonial boundaries. Even if he can be kind of a scary guy. Clive said, "if you're actually curious, read Marsha Linehan." Ok, I will.

I've been talking to Oothoon more, trans stuff is always such a mystery to me. But I'll bet in the future, guys like me will be trans whether we like it or not! Like, why be neither/nor? Why play a game to lose? I get it, but I'm way too dug in. I just watch and admire it in the younger set. Learning more about poetry has been a trip too. Lord Byron, man, he was a guy like Bill. Though maybe Bill's more down to Earth. But back to the other thing, I figure any guy who isn't packing heat is going to switch teams. God knows I would have as a teenager. Whatever. Other people's problems. Here's a joke: take my wife—

Please!

WOMEN

CLIVE POINTED OUT THAT I DON'T SEEM TO THINK VERY MUCH about women and that's true. Maybe I'm not taking them seriously. There's Mindy, and Oothoon, who's a transwoman, I think that counts. It definitely does. If you've got an attitude about that, take it elsewhere. I'm an ally. But basically, I live in a male universe. Most of my life is thinking about other guys, especially in the bedroom. What gets me off is male hierarchy and my place near the bottom of it. I think that maybe isn't very feminist, it kind of turns women into tokens in a game we're playing, but I'm not trying to be. My wife has a lot more fun than she probably would if I was a more "enlightened" guy. So, so much for feminism. Happy wife, happy life, I always said. So I found a lot of big strong guys to stick it to her. I think that's going pretty good.

I just wish the people in my life were easier to talk to. Clive is always talking online, he's kind of a frogman, it's all very right wing. Pepe this and Groyper that. Or maybe just against political correctness? I think they're against people. It freaks me out. Mindy isn't very online and neither is Bill. Me neither. I just read, I mean now that I've got some stuff to read. Oothoon is online too, but very ironic and ambiguous.

I should get to know more women, maybe my perspective is

fucked up. I guess I'm always a little afraid that they'll make me feel guilty for how I see the world. I'm really open to talking to everyone as long as you can respect me, as long as you understand that being a cuckold is not up for debate.

WANG DANG DOODLE

ARE THERE SONGS ABOUT BEING A CUCKOLD BESIDES "MR. Brightside" by the Killers? I guess there's "All You Ever Do" by Violent Delight. I wish more people listened to that band. Punks, but maybe they came to it too late to be punk. If they were twenty years older they'd be everybody's favorite band but then they'd probably be just as fucked up as me. But all of this stuff is too young for me. I could have never gone to their concerts. I guess Oklahoma, the musical. Some of that's implied.

A lot of the blues has these themes, I think. But that doesn't feel like my story to tell. What the hell is up with these white guys who get really into old blues records? They're so encyclopedic about it. Do you see yourselves? If I know one thing it's that it's not my story to tell. There's something I need to think through here, about being white. Like, am I just as racist as the guys who talk about being a cuck online? I don't think so. But I definitely do see what I'm doing as a white thing. I don't know why that is. Maybe I don't want to.

And boy, speaking of black guys, I should tell the story from our road trip of the night me and Mindy and Bill went to this Chicago style blues club in Reno. The guy, the singer, man did he have a swagger. Even Bill was sweating! All these guys, the alphas I mean, are kind of insecure. That's not the word. They're used to being Roman numeral one, numero uno, in any room, rumor is they're number one in the room, y'know? When they get the sense it might be otherwise they can't really cope. They never had to learn how. It's actually kind of cute, even when it seems aggressive. Like seeing dogs play.

Anyway, what can I say? We danced, even I loosened up after a few beers. Nobody expects white guys to be able to dance, but I've got my moves. In a way it's kind of goofy that I can't dance, I always feel like I'm getting attention for fucking up and then I wonder whether that's right. Is that fucked up? Then I freeze. High school all over again. All these black guys actually know how to dance, but I don't think it's from natural rhythm, I think it's because nobody thinks it's cute when they don't know how. They have to execute.

Well, the fun part came after the dancing. I'd been buying drinks for the band and we ended up playing a game of poker backstage at 3AM. I lost, like I always do. Mindy wins either way, to hear her tell it. She thought I threw the game. Not so, I wanted to go home and go to bed, if I'm remembering right. I don't especially care for fine powders. Instead I lost her to the band until morning. You know that Howlin Wolf song, about pitching a wang dang doodle all night long? I can't hear it the same way anymore.

ASTEROID

REMEMBER THE VOGUE FOR ASTEROID MOVIES IN THE 90S? IT WAS this funny moment of apocalyptic speculation about everything but global warming. I guess there was Waterworld, maybe I don't know what I'm talking about. Was that just the first moment of refocusing apocalyptic anxiety on something besides nukes after the Cold War? I read that on a blog once. I'm not a politics guy, so how should I know, but that sounds right to me. I'll see what Oothoon thinks. I don't need to speculate about asteroids. They're big and hard and can fuck up your world. I'm prepared for that. I know Clive.

I was thinking about a time when I was in middle school, when I got too cocky about science fiction. I'd been reading an Isaac Asimov book called "Foundation and Empire." I talked about it like it was real science and got called on it hard. What are the odds? I mean, I was eleven and this guy must have been thirty, and he was a science fiction fan. But to this day it smarts. Like maybe I should have died that day.

It's such an intense feeling. I remember thinking, "I'll never be a real person." And you know, I wasn't totally wrong about that. Sometimes I feel like a character in a book. I look at the solidity of a guy like Bill, the analytical precision of Clive or Derek, the raw energy of the bluesmen, Mindy's capacity for pleasure, Oothoon's <<je ne sais quoi.>> That's real. I don't think

I'm the way I am because of what happened to me as a kid, but I just feel like there's this hypersensitivity I've always had. This way another guy could make me feel like I'm not real. Even if he wasn't trying, and I don't just mean the bullies.

In regular situations I just crumple. According to Clive, borderlines do that too, they're very sensitive to rejection and invalidation, and fight with feelings of unreality and emptiness. Often suicidal, but not out of sadness, it's a way to get a grip on the situation. That sounds familiar, but all the stories in the stuff I was reading were way too extreme. I don't have borderline. Growing up meant learning to delay that crumpling reaction, shape it, so I don't just run home crying anymore. I learned to enjoy it sexually. I wonder what happens to guys like me. We're all kind of hiding in plain sight. Everything kills us, it's all too much.

When a guy is fucking my wife and they're both telling me how worthless I am, I guess that's the only time I really feel validated or seen. That crumpling feeling I was talking about before, you know. I used to get angry too, but now I don't get angry anymore. I wish I had more situations where I was allowed to be broken where I'm broken and it wasn't wrong to feel like I feel. I know I am broken. I need a shrink. Not Clive.

Clive is a creep but meeting him was an important step. He knows it, he's been in therapy for a long time, I guess. I guess it's common for therapists to also be patients. It must be weird to be like he is, kind of sharky, not really the same morally as other people. No empathy. But I guess he has feelings too.

He wants to be understood a little bit, and he wants to change a little bit. He says he has to be realistic about how much he can change and that that's the hardest part. I think maybe Clive has hurt some people very badly in the past, and that scares me sometimes. I don't know how much of what he says is true. But maybe I'm just prejudiced from too many crime novels, movies, et cetera. Clive is like the movie villains in a way, but he's a real person. He told me that "psychopaths" aren't even really a thing in psychology and I tried to look it up and got lost. I've been using that word my whole life and never knew what I was talking about, same as the science fiction.

Whatever's going on with me seems totally different. I'm so sensitive that I can never seem to hold it together. It's hard to imagine a life. I used to just get high when I felt like this, but I stopped. Now I don't know what. I'm just glad to have some people in my life who get it. If I lost Mindy, or Bill, or Clive, or Oothoon, I don't know if I'd have the energy to build a life again. Too many lives already. I'm worn down. Could you Hindu pranksters stop reincarnating me please, the joke isn't funny anymore.

I'm sorry to get heavy. Clive really got under my skin and I've been trying to process it. I should get back to my usual jokes and sex stuff and cuck philosophy. I'm just having a day. If a giant space rock smashed the Earth until there was nothing left, or we got ground into powder between two of them like a big millstone? That'd be bad but it might also be an answer to the big question mark I've got in place of a life. I'd get things straight for once. But you know what? Simpler isn't better. I'm not gonna be powdered sugar on a cosmic pancake. I'm gonna face my life and figure it out. I have people who care about me and we're going to make it. All of us together. I can take the waves.

SOUL

You know what absolutely sucks in 2017? People are scared to talk about the cuckolding lifestyle because they think it's right wing. We were here before all that! And God willing, we'll be here after. I'm not for any kind of hate, I actually believe love will win. Have I got some issues? Hell yeah, I wear them on my sleeve. But I'm just living my truth, or trying to figure out what it is. Same as anybody. Same as you.

I wish, I don't know, that I knew more people I could talk about this stuff with. Bill, Mindy, Clive? They get me, but they don't get it, you know? We all have our roles to play, and ultimately I feel like the cuck is the only one who thinks. It's more of an inner journey. It's deep. Maybe Bill is going pretty deep in my wife but that's not what I mean.

Oothoon is closer to getting it, but she has her own problems to deal with, and pretty good reasons to maintain boundaries with me. Plus she's far away. Plus she's young. Where on this punishment orb called Earth is a friend who's going through what I'm going through? I know you're out there.

I've been thinking some lately about what it's like for cucks who don't have wives. How would that manifest, even? Like, I see being a cuck as a really fundamental orientation, I think I was a cuck before I was married. But what does that even mean? I feel so blessed by having Mindy in my life and blessed again for being able to speak out about what's normally a very lonely and silent path. I mean, there's the forums but that doesn't count.

But the silent ones, the ones who faltered in their first steps on the path, or who never took one. What to say to them? I guess I don't know what to say and I don't really know what that's like. But I've been thinking about them today. Trying to think bigger than myself, and I don't mean—bigger—than myself. Maybe there are cucks who aren't even men. Is that postmodernism? I mean, obviously the situation doesn't make sense, but maybe they have the soul of a cuck. Maybe they're trans in reverse (is that a thing? like if a girl became a guy?).

If I ever write a book I might call it that, "Cuckold Soul." Oothoon said I ought to write a book. But who would read that? Who would publish it?

Speaking of cuckold souls, I think that water signs are the most likely to be in the lifestyle. I'm a Pisces sign, and I've seen a lot of Cancers. Scorpios love the dynamic but they're always the alpha as far as I can tell. I think I wouldn't believe in astrology if I wasn't a cuck and I never did before. I'm kind of a science guy. I'm team science. I only break out of that for music sometimes. Remember that old Sun Ra record, Astro Black? What if it was Astro Cuck. That'd be my theme music. Now I feel like one of those blues guys I was talking about the other day. I should shut up about black music. But I'm into Sun Ra, and I always kind of like that nobody expects that about me, like you expect to see a guy like me at a Mellencamp concert or something, and ok, Cherry Bomb is a great song. But nothing beats Sun Ra's Atlantis.

Here's a funny thing about that: if I'd gotten into this lifestyle through pornography instead of real life I'd probably be really racist like a lot of the guys online are. And I'd miss out on Sun Ra, I'd miss out on the bluesmen, probably, and I'd hurt a lot of other people's feelings too. The culture is fucked up. I think it's important for me to tell my story for that reason if no other. This shit is not about the color of your skin. Get over it. I always like to say we're one tribe. It makes me so mad. I mean, there are black guys who are like me, Bill is white, Clive is mixed. Who actually cares? But if you don't match the stereotypes it can lead to a lot of pain. From the black cucks I've met in forums some of it comes from their own group. I've got a friend online who's a black cuck, he says that the black community is really tough on him. Do real black people say "the black community" though? Who knows if people online are who they say they are, but it sounded real and just too sad. You need to let people be who they are. Move beyond the ignorance and the hate.

For me that means being a cuck. For you it might be different. But I'm not playing any games about this. I figure eventually some celebrity or rich person will come out as being in the lifestyle or be outed and then you'll all think that being a cuckold is cool. It isn't. It's just who we are. Here's the thing though, I'm going to remember who stood up for us when you didn't have to, when we weren't in the conversation as anything more than a punchline. And I'll remember who didn't.

Cuckold is the new Gay. And that I guess makes me Quentin Crisp or Oscar Wilde or Paul Lynde or something. I haven't thought it through. But I think I will write that book.

Mindy and Clive are watching the big speech and I just can't deal with it. I'm gonna go get a beer with Bill. Bill's a union guy, when he's got a job anyway. That's whose team I want to be on. The working man. Solidity. Decency. Caring about each other. I could never fathom getting too political though, it's not my personality. Political people already own the world, we need a place for us.

LESBIAN DEFLATION

MINDY TOLD ME SHE WAS INTERESTED IN EXPLORING RELATIONSHIPS with women. I feel surprised but without any real content to that surprise. Should I care? I just think I don't know what it is. I wonder if a masculine woman could play the same role that Bill or Clive does, or if it'd be a totally different thing. That might not even be the type she means. She likes masculine men. But then again, she likes me too, enough to marry me, even if it wasn't enough to be faithful to me. So all bets are off. Maybe I should have asked more questions. Maybe she'll bring home a rockabilly librarian with horn-rimmed glasses, a pin-up hairdo, bright lipstick, sailor tattoos, I don't know. Some lesbians look like that.

I guess I'm a little scared that the lesbians will convince her to get all feminist and decide I'm a pervert and our sex games were all for me. It's a recurring anxiety. Because really, anybody's more relaxed than me about this stuff. Her life could be easier without me. I worry about it with Bill too. It might not even be the lesbianism particularly, just doing something different, that's enough. She'll have some new perspective, and that's great. But it's hard to trust. Bill made her wanton. Clive made her mean. What's Cathy Granola Bulldyke gonna do to her? I guess I should revise that, she was exploring pleasure and she connected to Bill, she was exploring cruelty and limit experiences, and that led her to Clive. Nobody is "doing something" to her or making her some way that she isn't. That's a better way of thinking about it for sure, but it isn't any more reassuring. What's she exploring now? Guess I'll find out.

Anyway, Bill's a safe situation because he doesn't want to be tied down, he doesn't want the responsibility. I've never heard of the guy having a girlfriend or a wife in his life, and even if he did at some point, I mean, I feel bad for her. He doesn't seem to care about any of that. He's here for a good time. Plus he likes having me around as a sidekick. Would she run away with him? Sure. So would I. God, I'd love that. But he doesn't want that and we all know it. So it's ok. Bill's not going to run away with her, Clive's not going to murder us, the Craigslist guys aren't going to rip us off. God's in his heaven, all's right with the world. Everything is always sort of less dramatic than I make it. I can usually talk these things out, but I always seem to reach for the scariest interpretation first. I wish I knew how to stop doing that. It's related to the science fiction thing I was talking about earlier today, and it's all the same thing, I just don't have a name for it.

SIZE MATTERS

PEOPLE SEEM TO THINK THIS FETISH IS ABOUT DICK SIZE, AND IT'S not, or not in the way you'd think. I'm "average." I mean, average for the seventies, when I was born. When we're talking about dick in 2017 you have to understand that the ante's been raised. That five, six inches? That won't get you in the door anymore. Won't get you a seat at the big boy table where they play for keeps. But what I have is totally serviceable. It's the husband model, not the boyfriend model. And that's fine, I'm a good time, I'm told. Guys like Bill, Clive, Patrick, they're packing heat in a major way. Clive especially is almost comical. But that's not really the point. Probably a guy who was smaller than me could do the job, if he had the right attitude. Again and again: just get over the stereotypes. Well, maybe that's an exaggeration, you do need to bring something to the table.

I was talking recently to this alpha named Harvey and found out he's a total fake! He runs one of the alpha's perspective blogs, you know, these guys that have a blog all about their conquests of other guys' wives and girlfriends. Here's the thing, a lot of the blogs in the lifestyle are trying to sell you something or send you to some porn site, or they're really racist. It kills me to find out Harvey was a fake, you know, fuck the tourists. Maybe go write fan fiction, you fucking tool.

I'm for real. This is my life and struggle as a cuck. I don't mind role playing but people should say if that's what they're doing and should say who they are. I said really personal stuff to Harvey. So cool, some lady who works at a hospital knows all about me. Maybe the same hospital I was checked into for all I know. Be for real, people. Honesty counts. And don't assume we can all see the irony. We just see the face you show us.

I wonder if I'll find out Patrick or Clive or Bill is "ironically" fucking my wife, that he doesn't really mean it. Man, what the hell is wrong with people? I'm steamed this morning and I haven't even had my damn coffee.

GREG

SOMETHING'S CHANGED ABOUT MY WIFE. IT USED TO FEEL LIKE I was the one pushing for a lot of the cuckolding, but now she's doing her own thing. I like that, a little agency. She's got some attitude too, the way she swaggers around and picks up guys, girls, whoever. I think that's what I wanted. There might not even be a difference, maybe I'm psyching myself out, or she's ovulating and I'm making it into a bigger pattern. Who knows.

But she picked up a guy last night who I've got some history with, and she does too. Actually, I wonder if he isn't my son Tony's real dad. Or maybe you're supposed to say "biological" dad. Oothoon doesn't even like the word "biological." The only thing I'm sure of is that it's impossible to talk now, impossible to say what you mean, that's the world the young are building. No hope of staying ahead of it, but I don't want to be pigheaded either. What to do?

Anyway, Greg used to bully me in college. People don't understand how adults can bully each other but it totally continues. He actually broke up the one serious relationship I had before Mindy. Of course he's got the same attitude now that he always did. Mindy called me on the rotary dial during and passed on a message from him. "Greg says if you want him to wear a condom next time, buy bigger ones." I could hear him laughing at the old-fashioned phone in the background and imitating my voice. I don't really like it with him, he's too cruel. And anyway how to find bigger? I already buy these at the big and tall store, in the back. I'm looking online. These were even big enough for Clive, not that he ever wears one. I think it's just an attitude thing. All of these guys pull out anyway. Or they don't. That kills me. I can't stop thinking about it. If I was Mindy I'd never let a guy pull out. I'd need to feel it.

It's actually kind of cool that he found this way to channel being a bully. He's the perfect guy for this interaction, or he would be maybe if I was a little less sensitive, a little less reflective. I think there was more to the message but Mindy got nonverbal at some point and dropped the phone. It seemed like he started fucking her harder when I said "I love you," I heard his voice, "say 'I love you too,'" as he was pushing her over the edge. But she couldn't speak, just panting, moaning, dropping the phone. Greg always had a sense of humor. That would have worked for me if it wasn't so transparent, but I think in a way it wasn't as hot because Greg was so obviously focused on me the whole time. Still, I hope he comes around again, it definitely went better than I expected. And I hope Mindy doesn't go the lesbian route she's been talking about lately. I don't know. It's so weird to me. I am uncomfortable with it. I don't think that's homophobic. It's not very enlightened of me but it just freaks me out to think about Mindy as a lesbian. I won't stand in the way, just kinda hope she's straight. Maybe that isn't fair. I'm not ready for her to change.

Greg and I shared a double dorm in college and I had the top bunk. He'd get me stoned on hash and get me to admit my crushes. And every damn time, maybe the next night, maybe the night after, he'd bring that same girl back and nail her to the bottom bunk while I pretended to sleep or not to be there. One day to test a theory I mentioned someone I wasn't actually into and didn't actually know. Sure enough he fucked her for an hour and talked about his "loser roommate" a lot. I think it bothered her, because she knew who I was but we'd never exchanged a word. He made up stories about how I was pining away for her, and had clipped her picture out of the school paper and said it was mine. When she left, I just laughed.

I told Greg I knew he was only doing this because I named the girls. That his libido was broken, he couldn't take anything unless he felt like he was taking it from me, or from somebody else. He got really mad. He took me into the showers and beat the hell out of me with a rolled up towel. But he got caught! I thought he hated me after that, but we had some beers, and shots, a year or two later and I think it was fine. I say "I think" because I could really put them away when I was younger. I got too drunk back then, trying to play grown-up. I'd throw up. I fell out with most of who I knew then probably more out of embarrassment than anything else as I moved out of that phase. And I guess I lost track of Greg, hadn't thought of him in ages. I wonder if he's been thinking about me. I'm pretty sure our son is his, but you've got to figure a guy like that has probably fathered a lot of children. I don't know if that's even special to him.

KIT 1

I PREFER HIKING TO ROCK CLIMBING AND CUCKOLDRY TO "relationship anarchy." Is this just a generational thing? A friend told me to join a dating site and it's full of these "polyamory" people. I can't stand it. That's not what I'm doing. What I ought to do is try to find more transwomen like Oothoon. I pay attention to them online, and it seems like we've got some stuff in common, or at least they joke about it. Sissy or something. But it feels awkward to jump into a conversation, there's a kind of standoff there. Also they all seem to be fucking each other and don't take kindly to interest, even as they complain about no one loving them. It's a mess. Have you ever heard of a "chaser?" Apparently that's the name for a guy who likes them. Have you ever heard of a "bigot?" Apparently that's the name for a guy who doesn't. What can you do?

How do I acknowledge we're alike without saying that they're male or that I'm not? Gender is a fucking prison, man. Maybe I should get a rainbow hairdo and say that again, louder. Mindy would kill me, or maybe not since she's some kind of a dyke now. I do wish sometimes that I was childish enough to really live in trans world, but I'm mostly ok with what I can pick up from a distance.

Anyway, what's been going on with me? Not too much. Mindy met a butch woman named Kit and it's kind of a sweet but not at all charged dynamic for me. Kit just impresses me a lot. She's such a Real Person. She cooked us breakfast the other day and it was so solid and practical and perfect. None of my pretentious French sauces, this was hearty, cast-iron cooking. She's from the same Midwest workingman stock as Bill. I was a little mad at her the other day because she used my towel after chopping wood, but then again happy to have a cord of firewood split like that. And she just jumped in her truck and came back with towels and other stuff she needed to fix something with the engine. She's out there now under the truck messing around with something, maybe just changing the oil. I didn't need a new towel, I was just going to wash it. But now we have more towels, just a little thing that makes life better. She also told me to stop watering our plants so often, and the pampas grass already looks better. Kit's full of that kind of advice, and she always follows through.

I'm glad Mindy's happy and it's amazing to get to know someone like Kit, I mean normally how would I ever? It's bad enough that I'm a man, but in another way I'm not enough of one. It doesn't feel like cuckolding in the way that's hot for me, just like a complicated relationship. Kit asked me about my feelings and surprisingly shared hers. Under the gruff exterior she really gets people and she's so human. Again, real. Mostly I can't stop thinking about how I can never be like that. Though why is that? Could I? I kinda wish everyone in the world was a little more like her, but I know I'm not. Thank God I get to see Bill a little later. Guys night out or something, a little something just for the fellas, something for us, for once. Bill lets me be me. Kit's never been anything but nice to me but she sets off some anxiety, she makes me feel like a fake.

I always thought if I was a girl I'd have been straight. I mean, most are. For sure I wouldn't have been the Kit type. I'd have been pretty and passive, more like Mindy. But Mindy isn't really passive, she just likes to take it. I'm starting to realize that I'm a little bit jealous of her. Why can't I have someone like Kit, who's strong for me? And I mean, Kit is strong for herself. Her eyes are very gray and deep in a way that reminds me of Clive, but more human.

I guess Bill is sort of that, but it's such a schoolboy dynamic. I'm sort of his faggot, his lackey, or something. I always had friendships like that. I become some guy's sidekick and eventually the friendship falls apart when he gets a girlfriend, and we never put it together. That was youth. Again and again. I'd have said "I believe in male friendship." Sure thing, Walt Whitman.

I remember once trying to convince Mindy to be dominant, and it really didn't work for either of us. I said "Mistress Mindy" and we both started laughing too hard. Nothing to be done, maybe.

UNDER THE ROSE

SOMETIMES IT ANNOYS ME WHEN PEOPLE MAKE A JOKE OUT OF MY identity. Sometimes it's too funny not to laugh along with you. You know George Soros? What if it was the Open Marriage Society Foundations? I'll take my check for that one anytime.

It's funny that Clive has no problem calling people a cuck online and doesn't connect that to me, his friend. I guess I'm "one of the good ones." One of these days I'm gonna stand up for myself and say I AM NOT YOUR CUCKOLD. Metaphorically, anyway— metaphorically I'm not. Of course in reality I am, you fuck my wife and I love it and it reaffirms the order of men and women, of who we really are, of reality, that you're my superior, that you're a hypnotic vampire and we're all your drugged victims like cattle to slaughter.

But a part of me wants to stand up for all of us. We deserve, not dignity exactly, that goes against what this is, but I don't want to be a scapegoat for all the problems of society. I don't want it to be a slur. You know? I'm proud to be a cuck and I'm proud to be honest about who I am. Guys like Clive and his frogmen friends? They're not building a world where I can be happy or where I count. And what is the deal with the frogs anyway? I know about Pepe, but I always feel like I'm finding out about it, not really getting it.

I've been thinking since the election that maybe voting for

the Democrats and saying "I'm not a political guy," might not be enough anymore. Bill talked to me a little about a local group of socialists, which is a word that scared me, but I read some of their literature and it's got nothing to do with hammers and sickles and tanks and breadlines, except maybe as a joke. It's about what's been missing from the left, and maybe trying to steer it away from the college kids and back to the guys like Bill, or like Kit, though Kit's not a guy. I might show up to a meeting. For those who know, I'll see you in the streets. Under the rose.

KIT 2

M INDY'S FLING WITH K IT KEEPS GOING AND I JUST FEEL LIKE LESS
and less of a part of it. Fair enough. I wish I could belong to a
world of women, but I don't. I belong to whatever's beneath the
world of men, which some people think is the world of women,
but it isn't at all. How could anyone look at someone like Kit and
see that? If I thought women were weak, I would think that I,
who am weak, was a woman. But women aren't weak, Kit's living
proof. Some people are weak. So I'm in this null zone that has
no name, I've fallen out of masculinity, but I never landed, just
falling forever. I think I'm too much of a feminist to be trans. But
some women are losers too, what if I was like them? That's
something to think about, I guess. I can't rule that out. All the
women in my world are actually pretty cool. What would a
woman on my level be like?

They let me watch their sex this afternoon and I have to
admit that Kit does a better job with Mindy than Bill or Clive or
Patrick or Greg or any of the others. Different emphasis. But as
someone watching it's like, I don't have the same vicarious
athletic enjoyment. I said thanks and left after a little bit.
Watching Bill fuck my wife, that's like watching an athlete win
gold. Watching Kit is like watching a computer win a chess tour-
nament. Not because she does it without feeling, that's not what
I mean. It just seems so effortlessly great, but not in a way that I

can connect to even enough to activate my usually charged feelings of inadequacy. And that's what makes the thing go for me. That's the motor.

I know all of these other guys fantasize about lesbians but I don't get it. Like, what's your problem actually? I feel like when I think about that I just get a strong sense of it being none of my business. That's because it really isn't.

I do sometimes wish I had a more self-sufficient kink. Kit is enough for Mindy, and she can still have Bill, Clive, etc. whenever she feels like it. So where do I fit in? Maybe not at all. That scares the hell out of me, but not in a sexually exciting way. What if Mindy gets bored of me or of our games, what if she moves on? Am I supposed to remarry?

I'm imagining the pitch, imagining trying to date, when this is what I'm into. Evolving in this lifestyle has meant shedding a lot of illusions, and I don't think I could shut my eyes again now that I've had them opened. So in a way life is harder, even if it's sweet at the moment. Are there cucks out there meeting women and starting this kind of relationship on what, the third date? It's absolutely unimaginable to me.

I know about fetlife and okcupid but I don't know, I don't like it. I don't want to be that kind of fetish guy. I don't really believe in "kink" the way people seem to understand it. Lately I've been thinking it could be a spiritual thing. As long as there's a woman somewhere and a real man is giving it to her good. Does it matter if I know her? Maybe watching porn could be like getting cucked all the time. Maybe the guys who watch porn (I mostly don't except for pictures) are actually getting off on the feeling of being cucked by the stars. The celebrity divine masculine fucking the shit out of the celebrity divine feminine.

I'd feel like such a loser, though. What a way to spend my "forties." I've got to find a better way. I can't be this person I'm becoming. I'm sorry to get heavy. Maybe I ought to tell some stories from the old days or some of what Bill was telling me.

Oothoon was writing the other day about what it means to be a man now, how it's changed. But she didn't get to the part that hurts. What happens to guys like me, who are stuck with the old model of masculinity even as we're totally burned by it?

We lose a frame, even for our pain. I'll never be able to think of myself as anything but a loser, but nobody younger than me will really see why I feel that way, even if they agree for their own reasons. I look alright, I've got a beautiful wife, some money, a house, I'm in decent health. So what's my problem? I can't name the source of the pain, to them I'd just be a hysteric. But I guess that's not completely true, Oothoon is at least a decade younger than me and she gets it. I wonder what she sees in me, or whether I'm just a character to her.

EARLY MARRIAGE

A GUY LIKE ME HAS TO MARRY YOUNG, BEFORE THEY FIGURE YOU out. By 25 or 30, men have separated into layers. Oil and water and a layer in between. I never could have competed with guys like Bill and Clive, or with masculine women like Kit. Age 20, when I met Mindy, that was sort of the last sane moment we ever knew. It was the last time it felt like we were all the same and maybe I was gonna be ok. Well, I am ok.

I feel like there's a lot going on in everybody's life but mine lately. I ought to count my blessings, but it isn't all good. This doesn't feel like the same kind of adventure it was even a month or two ago. Doldrums, I guess. I have these dead times, I think any cuck does. I wish I had other cucks I could reach out to in person, and hope I can be someone other people reach out to someday.

When I was younger and felt this way, I think it made me change my life. More than once. I had to move, or I had to quit everything I was doing. That's why I went to college in Oregon, and never went back to Reno. I couldn't cope with the emptiness. Now? I'm too set in my ways, and besides, I learned to meditate. I feel like I'm watching myself from the outside sometimes, saying, "well, that's just how Darryl is." And I am.

We're supposed to believe in ourselves like we're always changing and to feel this sense of possibility. When I don't feel that I'm embarrassed. Oothoon suggested a line of Berryman's, that this was something like "admitting you have no inner resources." Henry was one hell of a gloomy guy. I don't want to be the mopey guy that sucks all the fun out of the room either. That's part of what's so nice about seeing a guy like Bill go at Mindy. He really knows how to enjoy life. He knows how to feel good. And everybody around him feels good. I wish I could make him feel good, but he mostly won't let me. He says it's not the same, he has to close his eyes to get off.

Maybe if I was better at it, I could practice I guess. How does a guy who's not gay get better at giving blow jobs? I don't want to watch porn, it's gross. But it's not really the mechanics, though, is it? I think it just makes him self-conscious knowing how I feel about it. It bothers him that I feel pathetic. It's actually empathy. He's got a heart, maybe too much sometimes. What I'd need to put on isn't skill but some kind of pride. But then I'd be gay.

That's ok for the rest of you, but I'm not gay. It'd be simpler if I was a girl. Maybe I should dredge up the dress I wore once last fall. You remember that whole mess, right? What a fiasco that was. But it could be better if I picked the clothes and didn't make such a thing out of it. Maybe if I wore something that was feminine but more casual, athleisure or what have you. Maybe no one else would even know. It could be an attitude thing. But I'd know, and maybe I'd feel better. I'll go to the mall I think, maybe up in Corvallis, I don't want to run into anybody.

CROSSDRESSING

THE IDEA OF "CROSSDRESSING" IS SO FUCKED UP, MAN, LIKE WHAT do actual women wear? Not big frilly dresses. T-shirts and jeans, yoga pants, fast fashion bullshit. So what's crossdressing? That's what I already wear. It's just an attitude. I like the frilly lacy stuff as much as the next guy but I'm not trying to support the petticoat-industrial complex. It's in the soul, man.

I could just be a little bit prettier, maybe I wouldn't say a damn word to anybody about it, and I'd just feel better. I'll bet Bill would, you know, let me make him happy sometimes. And it's March Madness, so we've got lots of excuses to hang out. Just, how to get him away from the other guys long enough? It'll be fine, "life finds a way," as they say.

"I can understand being a cuck, but why so flamboyant?"

PART 2: SPRING

CHRISTMAS

WHEN I STARTED READING LIFESTYLE BLOGS LAST YEAR, I NEVER thought that the alpha guys would eventually be writing me unprompted. But cuckolding is kind of a small world, and I guess my forum comments have been hitting home. Dreams really do come true! I feel like the luckiest guy in the world. I'm beginning to find a little bit of a voice about this stuff. I'm wondering if maybe I should start a blog, or a podcast or something.

Weird thought: how much of polite society depends on pretending that there are no true alphas, no bulls? How much of civilization? What's gonna happen when your wife finds out? What's gonna happen when you do? Do you think she knows that you know? It sounds like a caption but these are real questions.

If you're a cuck, you're not alone. There aren't all that many of us but I bet it'd be a lot more if people were more honest. And everything changes when you stop pretending, brother. Let yourself believe.

I remember on Christmas Mindy made me a card that was just my browser history with all of the alpha perspective caption blogs highlighted. I didn't get it but the present was this: these guys are the real deal (except for Harvey, as it turns out) and Mindy's going to meet them and let me watch. I hope the deal's still on now that Kit's in the picture. I have my inheritance so we can travel. I wonder how much is left, I should check at the bank. Between my hospital stay and Clive's bail, which now it sounds like I'm going to get back, or most of it, I'm not sure where I'm at. I've been irresponsible lately.

Thinking back now to Christmas Eve, I was wearing the sissy dress and Mindy sent me down to the pharmacy to pick up Plan B. No problem, I'll change. "No, like this." I had to go to four different pharmacies while fully dressed but I got it. I drove up to Corvallis but it was still humiliating. "No ma'am, it's not for me, it's for my wife, yes." Then I got this lecture about safe sex. I had to interrupt.

"Look," I said, "I always use a condom, and besides, I'm sterile."

"But why—" then she stared for a long time and checked me out.

When I got back, Mindy smiled and said, "if I'm gonna take this anyway I might as well get the most out of it" and called up Bill.

I guess I've been thinking about that day in the context of this revelation about cross dressing. Wearing that stupid dress was too much, but I don't think that's the kind of femininity that would make me feel better. I just want something subtle, a little change of attitude, cleaning up a bit. I'm gonna feel better and I'll bet I'm gonna vibe better with Bill. God, seeing him finish inside her that night, it's still the hottest thing I've ever seen. Why does that one detail mean so much to me?

It was a kind of a lightbulb moment. I'm so obsessed with this, maybe I need to feel it myself. But how? I didn't say anything at the time. Being gay wouldn't be any weirder than what I'm doing now but I also think I'd know if I was. But maybe I shouldn't think of it as "being gay," maybe I should think of it just as doing something. Taking Bill into my mouth doesn't feel gay. I don't know. For now it doesn't feel right, but maybe if I was dressed up it would. I like the thought of it feeling natural to him.

But yeah, what bothered me at the pharmacy wasn't the dress so much as the silliness of the dress. I think if I had more normal women's clothes it wouldn't feel humiliating at all, it could even be better. I could be the next Jenner. Well, I'm not a big city guy and I'm not that rich, even if the socialists say I am. I don't think it'd work out, I'm too old.

Maybe I'll get some more neutral clothes and try finding some guys online. Maybe some of Oothoon's "chasers." Finding the alphas was easy enough. I could use Mindy as bait. But could I even take it? Mindy used her finger once, but Bill is so huge, how does that even work? I wish I could stay satisfied with vicarious living like we've been doing. But it feels like I've opened Pandora's box, I already know I'm headed down this path. I already know that vicarious isn't enough.

I thought about whether I was gay in college and decided I must not be because like, I didn't think it'd be worth it if the guy wore a condom. And it was the early nineties, so we were all scared of AIDS. Real gay guys are into it anyway, even with a condom, because they're so into guys. But for me it's gotta be bareback. And that's too scary. So I just gave up. You think about weird stuff in your dorm room. I also used to listen a lot to Hawkwind, Yes, King Crimson, bands like that, and I felt like I probably couldn't meet a gay guy who liked that kind of rock, though I don't know why. I imagined they were all at the discos, but that can't really be true, can it?

MARCH MADNESS 1

I WENT OVER TO BILL'S LAST NIGHT FOR THE GAME. I WAS DRESSED a little different than usual in a way I want to describe. It was kind of my usual outfit but a little more relaxed, letting my body show just imperceptibly more through the clothes. I also shaved my arms, which had a subtle but for me tremendous effect. I don't know why that worked so much magic for me, it's not like I was ever a hairy guy, but I think it's similar to the way a room turns bright after you sweep the floor, even if it wasn't that dirty to begin with. I can't tell if they saw. There were some awkward moments, like when I asked Bill if he wanted another beer. I felt like all of his buddies were looking at me, maybe because I didn't ask them. Room full of guys, I should have said "I'm getting another beer, anybody want one?" Instead I think I said, "looking dry, Bill, want another?"

"Uh, sure, Darryl." I may as well have brought it to him on my knees. When I sat down next to him on the long couch, also, I felt their eyes. We bought him that couch and it's out of place here, too bright and new. Lotion-smooth like my arms. It isn't expensive but it looks expensive compared to what's around, the dinginess of this place. I could have sat a few man-widths away if I'd thought about it but I sat down right next to him, not even thinking about it, just the two of us on the left edge of the couch. Scooting away seems weirder.

When I left the room I heard a bit of conversation.

"He's a faggot, bro."

Then Bill's voice, "Come on, man. Darryl's my friend." I'm really glad to have a friend like Bill and wonder about some of these other guys, how repressed or whatever it is they are. And what does it mean that Bill's their friend? I started to feel like it'd look weird if I stayed past everyone else, so I left just at the end of the game, saying I had to get home to my WIFE. I said it very loud like that, stressed it. My WIFE. I said, "let me know if you're still hanging out later, I might be around," very nonchalant, and left, feeling the eyes again. I consider this kind of a failed experiment but I'm not giving up, just thinking about it. Like I almost think that those guys would have been nicer to me if I'd been wearing the Christmas dress.

I don't want to embarrass Bill. Obviously he's confident, he can take it, but I don't want to drag him through anything on my account. I basically don't belong in his world and I've got to remember that. I don't know. Maybe he'll say he can deal with it, and then at some point there's a breaking point, he falls out with his friends, and he blames me for losing them. Even if he thinks he can deal with that, he can't plan for how it'll feel. So I can't let it happen.

What's scary to me is that I can step just a little ways out, like shaving my arms and wearing a tighter t-shirt, and it's already too much for the boys. But at the same time, for Bill, I don't think it's anywhere near enough. He told me that when he's getting a blow job he doesn't really care who's doing it. That's cool but I want him to be able to open his eyes. I want him to see me and feel turned on. I want him to love me. I guess I never admitted that before.

I don't think he's going to, but I'm gonna find out. I wonder if a gay guy would? Probably, but now I feel a little bit like Bill myself. Or I feel kind of like those old fashioned gay guys I used to read about. They'd say "I don't want another queen, honey, I need a man!" Oothoon is like that too, though I always feel like she's putting on toughness, doesn't really want it like that, whatever she says. She says a lot about how people were more uninhibited and rougher back in the old days and talks like she wants to live that way, but I think I've got more experience with rough guys than she does. Is she just chicken? Sounds like she mostly lives in some kind of lesbian world with other transwomen. Whatever it is, I'm beginning to think nobody wants a faggot, not even me. But I'm a faggot and I'm not even gay. It's hell.

But hold on, it's not hell. This is something good I got from Clive, in spite of his psycho vampire shit. I need to break some of these thought loops, I get to feeling so doomed when the smallest thing goes wrong. I took a little step today and it didn't all go how I planned. But I don't want to write it off, nothing that was worth it ever worked right away. Shaving my body hair makes sense and I'll bet I could soften my body in other ways without setting off everybody's bells, just keep it subtle. I've been talking to Oothoon about this and she suggested I could do my eyebrows, my nails, tighter clothes, and maybe subtle makeup. I don't know. It all sounds like too much. I feel like she's trying to convince me to be trans, which kinda pisses me off. Like, she sort of has this script for how people are supposed to develop, we're supposed to "come out," and it's very one-size-fits-all. All the subtlety of Alcoholics Anonymous, "Admit your Power-lessness."

It helps that Mindy is some kind of a lesbian now, at least for Kit. But I wonder if she'd like a more feminine me. Probably not. Oothoon says people face this all the time and she calls it the Reckoning, she thinks—surprise surprise—, she thinks that they become trans after. It's such bullshit. She knew she was trans since she was a kid, and isn't that exactly how it's supposed to work. I'm in my mid-forties, if I was, I'd know. I was reading about "genderqueer" and I could probably be that but I also think most of the people who use that word, or about dozen other words like it, are my son Tony's age.

And Tony probably beats them up. I was thinking about that. He's a bully like his bio-dad, reckless, he's probably got some girl pregnant already. Well at least he's out of the house, and not bullying me anymore. A part of me hates him, like I hate his dad. Of course Greg would do that, and of course I'd be stupid enough to get married after, even though I knew. Well, maybe I should see it as a team effort. If she hadn't been pregnant I doubt she would have settled for me. She would have finished college and left me. Instead she's mine. The cost? Half my inheritance, a lot of my time, and raising a stranger's child. But what would I have been doing otherwise? Probably booze or business. I'd probably have moved back to Reno after college and lived with my parents. Heterosexuality makes me sick sometimes. Are these really the options?

Maybe I should call Tony up for advice. That'd be a funny reversal. "Hey Tony, it's your wimp dad, got any advice for sucking off the guys I share your mom with?" I don't think I should do that. I haven't tried talking to him. I remember talking to my mom about being a cuck when I was first excited about the lifestyle, last Fall, and it went really badly. She's old now, you can't expect someone that age to come around. But maybe "coming out" doesn't work. Do people come out to their kids about this stuff? I've heard of people transitioning gender on their deathbeds. Anything's possible. The main reason to talk to Tony about it wouldn't really be for me, it'd be to maybe teach him some compassion for the people he bullies. But that only works if he has any compassion for me. Greg doesn't, and I kinda think Tony doesn't either. I'm just a piggy bank to him. When was the last time he called without asking for money?

There's another game tomorrow and I'm gonna try hanging out with those guys again, but this time I'll play it really cool. I'll sit exactly the right distance from Bill and kind of ignore him. I'll wear a big sweatshirt but shave my whole body under it. None of these guys know anything. I don't believe they can see me. They never could.

Why does Bill put up with me? Like what's his deal? And why doesn't he ever have a girlfriend? I mean, he's always fucking somebody and about half the time it's my wife, but I've never heard of the guy being in a relationship. So he's different too. He doesn't talk about his feelings so much, so he's kind of a tough nut to crack. Crack it down my throat, maybe.

BRAD

I HAD A LONG TALK WITH MINDY AND KIT ABOUT BECOMING MORE sissy. I guess the deal is that they're cool with it, but they don't think it has much of a relationship to being a woman. I agree. I don't think they like the trans thing very much either but it doesn't matter, because I'm not. Kit had some pretty choice things to say about it. I think there's some kind of grudge between lesbians and transwomen, but wow, talk about inside baseball. Not my problem. But actually just seeing the disagreements set me free to explore this stuff a little more, like, I'm not necessarily wrong or unenlightened in how I see it, I'm just going to have one more opinion about this stuff, and there are a lot of opinions already. They don't really care how I dress, but they definitely agreed with me about avoiding the frilly "cross-dressing" looks. I'm glad they understand. Maybe the person I should really be talking to is Clive, he's a psychologist, sort of, he's probably got a whole theory of people like me, there's probably a word for it, like the borderline thing. I still need to think more about borderline because it does feel right in a way. But it's so frightening, like what are the treatment options? Half the books I find are about protecting yourself from being manipulated by someone who's borderline. But what if you are? How do you do better? How do you get better? It's like they don't care. Clive doesn't care either but that's because he can't care, not about me, or really about anybody. I learned a little more of his background recently and it's been freaking me out.

I guess Clive killed a guy as part of a sex thing a few years ago. There might be a video of it. What the fuck. He was a local guy, Brad Something, but it happened in LA. I don't know how I'd never heard of it, but I guess I don't exactly have my ear to the ground. He used to be pretty well known in fetish circles but now a lot of people won't talk to him or won't be seen talking to him. Knowing he's this all around sadomasochist gives me a little more sympathy for him. How would he have known the guy would bleed out? I think people might have been more understanding but for the fact that there was a tape, and the tape is still floating around. People try to sell it as some kind of "snuff film." Sick. That should be illegal if it isn't already.

I think the thing that ultimately isolates him is that he isn't traumatized. When you see blood, you've got to show everybody that you're shaken up, even if you aren't. But Clive is never shaken, and I think that makes people see him as a monster, even when he's the victim. Then again he doesn't exactly sound like the victim here, so maybe people are right. I don't know what happened but now I sort of think I have to find the tape. It's not that I want to see somebody die, I'd like to avoid that, but the chance to see Clive through a lens, I don't know, he's so much smarter than me. I want to see the side of him that he doesn't show me. I want to know what he looks like when he doesn't know I'm watching through a crack in the door, and when he hasn't drugged me.

I guess in retrospect this explains why his bail was set so high a couple months ago. But hey, I got the money back, so I'm feeling pretty flush! I'm going to help Oothoon get surgery, her insurance won't cover it. Even if they did, there'd still be all this money you have to spend on recovery, and the insurance always fucks you in the end. This is why I've been moving to the left. Our healthcare system is sick, sicker than Clive even. I think Mindy would get mad at me if she knew I was going to give a lot of money to Oothoon and what it was for. But you know what? It's my money. She forgets that sometimes and so do I. I've never spent a big chunk all at once except for the house, not even once. She can't stop me from giving it away. I wonder if Mindy knows anything about Clive's past. I wonder why he told me. Now that I know what I know about him, it feels like I'm sharing a secret with him. I don't like that feeling. The only thing I want to share is my wife! And I guess my money, but not with Clive.

MARCH MADNESS 2

I WENT TO BILL'S TO WATCH ANOTHER GAME, THIS TIME JUST ME and him. I hope he gets a job soon but it's cool that we've got the afternoons together. I asked him if it bugged him how I was the other day and he said no, that his friends were just being jerks. I think I believe him, but I think he still hasn't put it together that his friends are always going to be that way when I'm around. He's never had a real sissy friend before me, I think, so he's like a "virgin." He thinks he can have it all. I don't know much but I know I can't have it all. Though I guess I don't know that for sure about Bill. I feel like Bill would be the kind of guy to tell you at some point randomly that he had a boyfriend for a couple years like it's nothing. If he did, he'd be totally cool about it, he wouldn't make anything weird, not swishy, not in-your-face. Bill's not defiant, he's solid. But I don't think he has.

The game was good. It's hard for me to get into college basketball, it's not as theatrical as the NBA, and I'm really there for the drama and the dance of it. I think college ball is more for people who love the game. I just love the bodies, I think about how maybe with one enormous hand one of these guys— I mean, have you ever met basketball players up close? I knew some of them when I was at U of O. I think there's no way to ask this without sounding racist but why are there so many black guys? Maybe just a neighborhood culture of playing basketball?

And they're so absolutely beautiful and intense. I don't want to project anything. I don't know. Why does life have to be so complicated? Every time I try to give a black guy a compliment I find I start to suspect myself of being racist. Is what I'm saying ok?

During halftime I asked Bill if he knew the story about Brad and he kinda froze. "Yeah, I knew him." I asked if he knew how he died and he said he didn't want to talk anymore. I guess Bill and Brad had been close. Then I remembered what Bill had said around New Years, that he had a friend in some fetish lifestyle who died. Is it possible it was the same guy? I was too high to take in the story.

The thing about "triggers," I was reading about this online, is that it's really not worth it to dig. Like it's kinda hard to know what's going to make Bill feel a lot worse, or what's going to take him into it. I confess to being really curious but I'm going to look at the obituaries in the Register Guard, it might be a trip to the library. I could finally look at those Berryman poems too, while I'm there.

After the game, Bill said I could take his mind off it and closed his eyes. He said he liked it better now that I was smooth, and just as he was about to cum he said, "I love your mouth." I can't get that out of my head. It's such a small affection and it meant everything. God I wish he'd just fucking fuck me. I don't even know how to do that, do you have to clean up somehow first? I should look that up too. I remembered how I felt when I asked him to hurt me, in December, and how hurt he was by that, and everything rotten and broken in the situation and I didn't say anything. But at the time I didn't know how bad that was.

Anyway, my team won, I picked Charlotte just as a joke because I know Bill likes competition. I like it too, but I want Bill to win all the time. Or maybe not, just enough that it feels real to him. I was thinking the whole time about how it would have been if we were in high school and I was a cheerleader and he was a jock, he must have been a jock. He probably fucked a lot of those girls really good. Can you imagine how hard he used to go, if this is what he can do now? What that would be like? What would it be like to be her? I want a pony, daddy! And it's a Clydesdale. I'm so horny I could explode.

You know when I'm thinking about it on my own I always think that my pleasure doesn't matter but I wish I could cum sometimes, with Bill. That'd be gay though, maybe too much. We'll figure it out.

LIBRARY

I TOOK A TRIP TO THE LIBRARY, IT TURNED OUT THAT MOST OF what I needed was on the computer but I'm glad I didn't use mine. I don't want this kind of stuff in my browser history. First of all there were a lot of articles about what had happened, back in 2004. It scandalized Eugene. Everybody had to learn all at once about the existence of this hardcore fetish subculture and that someone had died in it. That's not a great impression. But also, I think people love these stories and it's just sick. I wonder how they would have felt if I'd died in January, whether that would be a story for them too. Everybody's got a favorite serial killer. Or they talk so lightly about people who OD on drugs, as if being famous or having a pill problem makes your life not a life. Sometimes humans aren't very human.

It's really hard for me to get a picture of who Brad was because everything is just one conversation after another about "what is BDSM?" or "what is Craigslist?" or "what's a snuff film?" I feel like there's really a story here and it's not in the Register Guard or any other paper. One thing that is clear is that there's more of a scene in this town than I ever knew, and it's more connected to the shit going on in LA, Seattle, wherever. A lot of the guys I've been finding for Mindy are from there. And there's less of a separation between gay and straight than I thought. I wonder if they know about it.

I found some escort forums. What I'm seeing there is that Brad, whoever he was, was a hustler, he was a boy for hire in LA, but sometimes came back to Oregon when he was down on his luck, so pretty often. He was a lot younger. He also didn't always go by Brad. And there might have been more than one Brad. I didn't know what to make of that. You can't trust forums, think of how it went with Harvey the so-called alpha, people love to talk tough. But this was different. People on the forum put his age anywhere from 15 to 19 but the obituary said 22. That still checks out, everybody lies about their age. But I still have so many questions. Why did Bill have a friend that young? Brad was about a decade younger than me, and I think Bill's a little older. And Brad was one of those little blonde gay guys, a "twink." Just yesterday I was thinking he didn't know what it was like to have sissy friends, that he didn't know how to do it. Now I'm totally confused. Bill, Clive, they were part of a gay world, at least peripherally. Gay underworld, really. Most gay guys don't go anywhere near this stuff. But Bill had someone he cared about there, and Clive had someone he destroyed.

The story I'm picking up is that Brad had an older boyfriend named Brian, who he was sort of the prisoner of. He was rented out by the hour for more and more severe scenes and often they made videos. Eventually, they went too far, and killed him by accident, or maybe not by accident. It does seem like if anybody was going to make a snuff film it would be these guys, and that if anybody could do the deed it'd be Clive, but I also think everyone on this website is lying. So I don't know what to do. I feel like I ought to ask Clive, or his friend Derek, the lawyer. What happened to that guy? Is Clive Brian? Too horrible to contemplate.

I'm very frightened of this situation, but there's a feeling of being doomed by my curiosity, reminds me of old movies. Pulling into the mansion on Sunset Blvd. I don't want to ruin my life but I want to understand what happened. I always catch myself thinking these very paranoid things about Clive, for example that he's an actual monster, that he's Hannibal Lecter. Then I think: no, that's nonsense. But I'm beginning to see now that some of my instincts were right. It's not that I'm so worried he'll do anything to me but he really is the predator I've been imagining. Or he used to be. Was he defanged somehow? If so, how did he change? Do people who go that far ever change? How have the lion and the lamb's wife come to lay down?

MARCH MADNESS 3

I WENT TO BILL'S FOR THE FINALS. ACTUALLY, I DROVE US OVER since he'd spent the night with Mindy and he had the guys coming over in the afternoon. I woke very early and before breakfast I did what I'd planned. I got myself cleaned up and even cleared my unibrow with these special tweezers I picked up at the mall. I have to be very careful not to accumulate too much of this stuff, because Bill is the type of guy who uses everything in the bathroom. I always notice, because I remember the orientations of things. So I see when everything's been taken out of the cabinet and placed back, or the bottle of lube is down half a finger, or the toothpaste tube is unrolled, even if it's rerolled. That's the one way he's not polite, and it's such a small thing that instead of getting mad about it it just makes me love him more. Maybe that fine awareness is genetic. I wonder if my parents could tell when I was younger, dad's whiskey down an inch or infinitesimally watered down, mom's summer dress hastily stuffed back into the drawer, half the quarters gone from the change jar. That's alright, I'm alive and beautiful underneath my clothes. Heavy gray sweatshirt that I once thought of as fitting me, back when I'd just mindlessly say "yeah, give me the large." And now I'm thinking, "yeah, give me the large." I'm thinking about it and it feels good, like nobody knows that I'm wearing

my boyfriend's clothes. I like that idea of myself, hidden under a
baggy sweatshirt. My light is like that. For a second I could see it.

I wrote to Oothoon again about this and of course she thinks
she's got the skeleton key to reality as usual, everything is trans
to her. I'm so frustrated by that, I told her so. I feel like I'm being
pulled into some kind of cycle of hazing there. I know she talks
to her friends about me. All these people do is recruit and
they're all in bed with each other. In a way that doesn't sound so
bad, but I already have a life and besides, I'm a little older, and
way out here in Oregon. What am I supposed to do with the
under thirty set?

Anyway, I helped Bill get set up and then made a point of
getting out of there. The thought I had was that his friends had
better not get the impression I'm always around. It's funny how
unselfconscious he is about all of this, I'm more scared for him
than he is for himself. Maybe I'm scared that when they start
giving him a really hard time he'll drop me. How do you trust a
guy who doesn't know himself? I don't know. I don't know
myself either. And maybe he knows himself better than I think.
Is Bill nice to me because I remind him of Brad in a way? I feel
more and more identified with that guy without ever having
known him and all I know about him being things that aren't
like me at all. He had a narrow, feminine body, he was blonde,
he died young, he'd let people use him. None of that is me, not
even the last one, though there's something very beautiful about
it, the idea of floating peacefully away while some creep wrecks
my body. I guess the creep was Clive. Clive fucks guys? Does Bill
even know Clive is in the picture? I always avoided his name.
"Mindy's other boyfriend is a real jerk." I remember saying it
like that a few times. Mind swirling with questions.

I couldn't figure it out but I laid out some bowls of chips,
some Chex mix, and filled the fridge with beer and soda. All in
straight lines. Then I worried that maybe if it was too neat they'd
start asking Bill if he got a maid, or a faggot friend. So I spilled
some of the Chex mix over the side of the bowl onto the table.
Bill asked why I did that and I said it was wabi-sabi, and messed
up the beers too. I learned that word from Clive, it means incor-

porating a little bit of imperfection and asymmetry, Japanese style. "Like your sweatshirt?" I love him.

I didn't have anything to do so I headed back to the library to learn more about Brad. I decided that I had better get in touch with the local BDSM chapter, there's something called a Munch and I'm gonna check it out soon. It's funny that now of all times I'd finally get in touch with the fetish community at large after being disgusted for so long with them. "Oh, Darryl, you've decided we're ok now?" No, I'm here because I think you're killers. I have to understand what you did to Brad. I can't say that to them, I can't say that to anyone. But I'm going to look out for the old heads and see if someone can tell me what's going on.

I came back with a lot of ideas in my head and played my part perfectly at the game. I was Mr. Bro, so distant from everything. I remember feeling like I was betraying myself. I leaned into a heavy "fuck yeah!" and let my voice really resonate deep when I saw a layup. I thought, well, there it is, my old love of power and the masculine. I can't tell if I'm exactly like these guys or exactly the opposite. It's all vicarious but it means something else for them. I didn't sit next to Bill, I didn't get him beers, it was like I didn't know him. But I lingered a little while after and he asked me if I was angry with him. I don't know what to do. I love him so much and I can't win. I wish Clive would come along and kill all of these stupid brutal straight guys, except Bill.

Something special this time was that I didn't feel like I had to wheel and deal to get Bill into my mouth, he seemed like he'd come to expect it. I thought selfishly that maybe he's hooked now, he won't let his little sissy bitch go without a fight. I wonder if he misses Brad. I wish we could talk about that but I didn't want to press. He actually started to bring it up himself and I shushed him, said he didn't have to. He seemed relieved. Then I gave him some real relief.

DOG

CLIVE AND BRAD ARE ALL I CAN THINK ABOUT THESE DAYS, EVEN when I'm with Bill. How did I come to let the devil rule my world? It isn't right. I spent an afternoon with Mindy and it was so nice, it feels like something's changed and we're going to make it. That's Kit's influence maybe, but maybe that's selling ourselves short, we've really grown. It wasn't so many months ago that we were thinking about divorce, but it feels like that never happened. We've been carrying on just forgetting that I ever ODed, forgetting the hospital, forgetting the ways we were egging each other on into the lifestyle just last fall. Just carrying on carrying on. But we were so close to falling apart. I asked her if she thinks about that stuff and she said she hadn't thought about it in a while, but that it felt like a moment that had passed. Actually I feel the same way.

What I didn't feel ready to talk about was the way I've been feeling about Bill, and how I almost don't feel interested in being a cuck lately. Was it all a phase? No, it's still hot. But maybe it's less interesting? Right now I feel like I don't care whether I'm enough of a man for Mindy or anybody else. I'm aimed at something different. And besides, I'm starting to see my feelings less through a lens of competition, there's not even a goal. I'm just being, just me. I sound like a hippie.

Before, it was about seeing the drama of it again and again, it always felt like a revelation. These days, I'm just jealous of Mindy. I actually bought some toys to work up to that, but it doesn't feel at all like I expected. Sometimes it hurts, sometimes it feels like nothing at all. I don't think I'm doing it right. It feels like it would take a lot of working up to and I wonder if Bill could stay hard that long. Who am I kidding, of course he could. It's just whether he wants to. But I don't want to push him too far. Same as with his friends. The fear is that he "comes to his senses" and he's not in his comfort zone, and I'm to blame.

Mindy and Kit are going to visit Kit's daughter, she's graduating college in Western Massachusetts somewhere. A trip that long makes me think they must be getting pretty serious but then again I think that's just how lesbians operate. The daughter is a dyke too, probably studies gender or something. That seems like a vicious enough irony. I wonder if she knows Oothoon online. I can't stop thinking about this John Berryman poem she showed me, Henry staring at a woman across the restaurant while she's "filling her compact & delicious body with chicken paprika." Why do we hang onto a line like that? I don't think Henry's so deep, he's just a mopey forty-something guy that wishes he was black, wishes he was sober, wishes his dad were still around. Hmm. Ok, that's relatable. But he's too into culture, what can you do with poetry? It doesn't matter. We should be writing songs, or blog posts or something. Something people read.

Mindy had to run and meet Kit and surprisingly I felt I couldn't wait for her to leave. I was sort of outside watching myself feel that, like in meditation. I wanted to take a long walk and I wanted to think and I wanted to try again with the toys I bought. I was so anxious about losing her but once the anxiety cleared, it's like I didn't have anything to say. Maybe cuckolding blew out my eardrums like a rock concert, regular emotions are too quiet now. She didn't have much to say to me either. When she left, I put on Hawkwind, Space Ritual. I took a long walk after and a dog followed me.

This was a funny thing to happen, there aren't a lot of stray dogs around here. I checked for a collar and didn't find one, thought about taking it to animal control, but figured he'd probably find his way home and shooed him off. But as I kept walking, I kept seeing that dog and wondering if I'd done the right thing. Eventually, I realized he was following me, and not too long after that he was trotting along by my side. I'd made a friend! Alright. It struck me how rare that is, I think we sort of live in a world where to be truly grown up means not having any friends, you just eat, drink, sleep, fuck, work, that's what being a man is. I'm exempt from a lot of it because of my inheritance, which is maybe what lets me be such a sissy. But the dog doesn't care, he's just glad to have a place to go and someone to be with.

But here's the thing. Just as I was crossing 7th, where the highway comes down near Washington, the dog ran right into the road and got hit. I thought for a moment that he might have died and just felt awful, I don't know why I assumed a street dog would know where he was going. Probably wasn't even a street dog, just somebody's runaway, off on an adventure that ended too soon. Hit and run too, but what am I supposed to do, call the cops? "Yes, officer, a white dodge — no, I didn't get the plates." But to my surprise he managed to get up, shake himself off, and trot over to me, tail still wagging. Thank God. I leaned down and kissed his face, I just let him lick me all over my mouth, which I've never done before but is actually fine. I've heard this is supposed to be a white thing, and ok, I'm a white guy. I can show affection. I kiss dogs on the mouth. I said "you damn dope, let me buy you some dinner."

I motioned for him to wait for me outside of a burger joint and I asked the girl behind the counter what dogs eat. "Hamburgers. Mine loves 'em." This was one ugly girl, very masculine features and it struck me that most of the time when I think about women, I'm thinking about pretty girls. Men too, it's all hashed out in ideal types. I wanted to say to her that seeing how ugly and really gross she was, and how poor, to be working at this burger joint and still doing it, it made something feel possible for me. That there'd been a little motion in my heart. But isn't that just condescending and mean? Better not to say anything. So I said a burger sounded pretty good to me and bought two, well done, one plain for the dog and one with a lot of pickles and mayo for me. I unwrapped the plain one and held it out to the dog, who sniffed it for a little while, looked up at me, then ran as fast as he could in the other direction! It's too easy to lose a friend. I'd have taken care of that dog every day of its damn life. Where'd he go?

MOTHER

I MANAGED TO PAGE CLIVE ENOUGH TIMES THAT HE CALLED ME back from a payphone, audibly annoyed. I find that really funny, there must be only one or two payphones in town and I haven't used one myself since the mid-nineties. I remembered a prank I did as a kid in Reno, I had a little telescope set up in my room and I'd memorized the number of a payphone that I could see from my window. As a stranger was walking by, I'd call it, and just let it ring. Sometimes the person would pick up. Most often I'd just dissolve in giggles, or try to say something scary, or do some heavy breathing. "Surrender, Dorothy!" There was a movie that I learned the heavy breathing thing from, "Little Murders." I don't know why I've never met anybody else who's seen it, but I remember identifying a lot with Elliott Gould's character, he was so sad and wise and hopeless, and really funny. Why did I want to be like that, anyway? Pink Floyd had it right man, "no dark sarcasm in the classroom." I asked Clive if we could meet for coffee and then remembered that he doesn't drink it. He doesn't take any intoxicants at all but he always seems to have something around, just the right pill. And you don't ask any questions, you just take it.

We're going on a hike instead, up Mount Pisgah. That lets us have a private conversation, which is hard to do in a town like Eugene, where it feels like I know everybody. And who knows how many people are in the lifestyle here. I don't think Clive is working with another couple, but he easily could be. There could be another Darryl, another Mindy.

I find everybody in Eugene is full of secrets, that's Oregon. Clive most of all. I don't know if I want to be alone with him. Somehow on the phone I told him about my meditation. He said, "nobody meditates." What does he mean by that? I found myself spontaneously telling him everything about how I was changing, how I was beginning to see the world in a different way. "I want to live, Clive."

"I know."

Clive knows everything, so that isn't saying much. I wish he'd said that he agreed, that cares about me too. But I think that's as good as you get from him.

The plan is to meet on Wednesday at two. I feel so lucky to have a group of friends without real jobs, it makes me think back to the novels I read in college. For a while I was trying to be a very serious book guy and got interested in Henry James, or tried to. None of his characters ever work, I think. They're off to Italy to take in the afternoon light, or look at frescoes. I don't even know what a fresco is.

I sort of feel like whatever my cuckolding group is, we belong to the nineteenth century, or to a vanished aristocracy. I guess in a way we are aristocratic, literally. I live this life because of who my dad was and the fact that he died young. Both essential. I don't think that if he was still around he'd have given me an allowance in my forties. I'm a grown man. Maybe he'd show mercy but I'm sure I'd have been cut off at some point, just long enough to have to find my way, make a little money, show him that I could be like he was. That's the kind of guy he was. I probably would have reminded him more of the guys he was always complaining about, the ones he had to fight or had to fire. It's a man's world, he'd say, but in a brittle way. I don't think Mom ever loved him.

I was thinking recently that maybe if my mom had a chance to have more of her own life when she was younger, she'd have been a lesbian like Kit. Or maybe not, I don't want to be like Oothoon, seeing sexuality behind every door. After Dad died, I think she never had a friend that was a guy. She just kept having these intense female friendships that would burn out after a few years, like maybe something was supposed to happen that didn't. The friendship would deepen and they'd hit a wall. I'm not there, I don't know. I don't want to think about my Mom in a sexual way so I don't worry about it, but sometimes I worry that she seems very lonely. She told me on the phone that she was lonely, and afraid to get old like that. She said she was worried that I was crazy, and that she'd seen my life change too many times, and that nobody else knew me the way she does. That kind of stuff. I never told her when I was in the hospital, but I think she must have known, because she started calling a lot after. Did Mindy say something? We talk about twice a week, and every time I think it makes me feel worse, but nothing would be worse than stopping. We're both very lonely people when I think of it, and it scares me to end up like her, or like she's probably going to end up.

I used to hike all the time, that was sort of who I was. When I say I'm not a nature guy, it's because I'm not into the sport of it. But the feeling's there. When I'm in the woods I start to get this feeling of life, I start to see the whole forest as one living thing. Then I start to see the human species that way, as a tree whose roots maybe don't go down so deep, and whatever this tree is, I must be a dead leaf of it. What if everybody else is a live one, or a pinecone, or a nut? What are they going to do when they find out about me? Pruning time.

There's three trees by the river, a little flushed red one, a big towering green one that seems to hold it, and a little green one facing but separate, further down. I remember walking by in Fall and saying "I guess that's Mindy, Bill, and me." I can't see it any other way now. I don't know why I can still feel the pain about this when I've moved on so far from that revelation. Of course I'm not a big leafy man like Bill is, that's why I love him, that's why I'm different, whatever way it is that I'm different. But I can't seem to move on from that picture. Does that make sense? I said this to Clive and he seemed not exactly bored but he always seems to have predicted in advance what I'm going to say and almost seems to have decided it. How does that control work? I find I'm more and more fascinated by him.

I really need to keep one thing in perspective here, which is that Clive is not an ok guy. I don't understand or believe any of what supposedly went on with Brad, but I know I'm out of my depth. I can only get so close to that. Meanwhile, I figured out what sounded familiar about Brad's last name. He was Bill's half-brother.

PART 3: SUMMER

MUNCH

I WENT TO THE MONTHLY EUGENE BDSM & POLYAMORY MUNCH. Are you proud of me? Ashamed? I'm ashamed of myself. But not really, to my surprise, I actually had a great time. And it was nice to learn a little more about the history of the movement, even if it's all very San Francisco. I generally hate anything that comes out of San Francisco. What do the Society of Janus or the Exiles have to do with me? What does that mean in Eugene? But I learned the basics and I met a lot of guys my age that were dominant or submissive or whatever. I said that I was married and "exploring, with permission" but preferred not to give any details about my situation, actually nobody even asked, and thank God for that. What I said was pretty much true anyway, even if it isn't totally honest. Mindy knew I was going. And you'll never guess who was there: Patrick, the biker! He ended up giving me a ride home on the backseat of his hog and I've never felt so alive. What am I saying. The point isn't to compare. He took me on a long detour out of town, through Coburg, my eyes were just streaming with pollen, we must have gone about eighty miles per hour, and actually passed my aunt Farol's house.

I guess Patrick is pretty well known as an organizer of local BDSM events, guess that explains why it was so easy for him to get all of those biker guys together for the gangbang last month.

He's a real diplomat in this world. And I guess he's in an "open marriage" with Satori who runs Awaken, the tattoo place that doubles as a yoga studio. I've walked by it a million times and even spun the Tibetan prayer wheel once as I was passing by. Maybe it'll work.

Patrick calls sex "play." I don't get people like that but I'm starting to think I might like them. We stopped for a bit by the McKenzie river and I asked him if he ever knew Clive. He got a bit quiet and said that he'd known Clive a few years ago, and then he asked me if Clive was back in town. Nobody wants to tell me what they know. It's clear that Clive was part of this community fifteen years ago and that he was very well known. Apparently he was one of the hardest "players" on the West Coast at one point. But what did it mean?

I asked if he knew anything about Brad, and whether he thought Clive had killed him. He looked off into space for a long time before answering. "I think Brad wanted to die. I don't know any more than that." But he said a little more. Apparently Brad was very sick and would have died anyway. I can't decide if that makes things better or worse. Definitely worse. It seems like this whole town knows about Clive and is scared of him, but nobody will say a word, it's like they all share a secret. But as we were riding home Patrick told me that Clive used to go by a different name, Brian, which put a bunch of pieces into place. Clive wasn't brought in just for the video, he was actually Brad's older boyfriend or handler or master or whatever that I'd read about on the forum, who'd been pimping him out and selling the videos. So who was the ringer? Derek? Always more questions than answers.

I have to remind myself that I'm not a detective, and that I don't have a reason to uncover any of this stuff. In fact it might be dangerous to. I almost feel like I'd better tell Clive that I got curious and that I'm done being curious now, I'll settle right now for whatever he tells me. I don't want to know any more. The worst way this could go is to get either too deep with Clive or any closer to a situation that makes me lose Bill, or Mindy. It's surprisingly hard to do this, to get comfortable not knowing. But I think I'm ready to stop exploring this for a while. I have to put everything back the way it was, so it looks like I never peeked at it. Dad's whiskey again. Mom's dress.

As for the BDSM, it mostly just seemed pathetic to me. I felt like I'd been exactly right not to explore it for most of my life. It's sort of like bumper bowling as far as the emotions that are actually in play when I "play" with Mindy. For us it's not a game at all. It's about the truth. I felt like I had the most in common with the guys who were dominant, not because I am, but because they were so obviously looking for a sandbox situation where they could be men again, accepting that they couldn't be in real life. I've accepted that too, but I follow through. I wonder how Clive relates to this. It seems strange to be so right wing and to have a connection to all of this deviant sex, but maybe it isn't. Maybe Clive decided at some point that he was interested in real power and real violence, and that means politics. I saw his bedroom for a second once: very clean, bare white walls and a portrait of Suharto. Is he related? It made me wonder about all the great men and all the terrible ones who've made our world, or marks on it. Were they getting off on it all along?

ROUGH

MINDY HEADED TO THE AIRPORT AFTER A QUICK SESSION WITH Greg, who was surprisingly rough with me. I let him in and he sort of pushed me to the floor with one motion and spit in my face. I couldn't stop giggling. He crouched over me, pulled out his dick, which was already hard, and growled, "remember me?" I'm too old for this, and I know I'm going to bruise up. He gave me a corny lecture to the effect that my wife was his whore, and sort of marched into the bedroom, tracking dirt across the carpet. "Get over here, you little bitch," he motioned to Mindy. She walked over and whispered something to him. He seemed very distressed by what she'd said, then in a matter of minutes actually left! I couldn't believe it.

According to Mindy, what she'd said to him was that hitting me wasn't part of the deal, and neither was calling her names. Apparently a lot of these guys ask if they can beat me up or get me to suck them off or something. She always tells them no. I never thought of it, it just goes to show that I shouldn't assume these guys are all totally straight. Maybe they even are, but they'll color outside the lines for a sissy, as part of a scene. As long as it's violent, I guess. That's how boys do it. I think it's funny that none of them ever thought to ask me directly, I'd probably have let them. I'm beginning to think that no one wants my two cents anymore. Nobody consults me about anything.

I asked if Bill had ever asked to do stuff with me and she started giggling.

"I know about you guys."

"Oh."

I guess I hadn't thought about how obvious it all was. I asked her if she knew about Bill's half-brother and she said that she didn't talk about emotions with Bill, but that she did know that. I asked if she knew it was Clive who killed him and she went very silent. She said that Clive doesn't talk, which is true and it's not. Every time I talk to Clive I feel like I've told him everything and he's told me nothing. I feel I'm on the verge of something here, the curiosity about him that I keep trying to suppress. It still has something to tell me. Should I be more scared? I mean, we're talking about murder, or manslaughter or something. Is Mindy safe. She says he didn't do it, but how would she know?

I started thinking about how badly I wanted to see Greg let loose inside her in that moment, what a rough fuck he tends to be, and I wondered about that impulse. Do I want Greg to hurt her? To defile her? Do I want those things for myself? I feel like with the toys I'm battling a constant fear that I'll rip or break or something, until I get into it and then it seems you could throw anything in there. Drop an anvil on me like a cartoon, I'd just accordion back. I don't know myself as well as Mindy. But the experience of getting fucked, even just by my own toys, is changing how I think about what happens to her. Nothing's the same as it was when we started.

I told Mindy that I wasn't afraid to get fucked anymore and she offered to try it with the strap-on right then and there. Ok, I am scared. I wasn't ready but we'll try it when she comes back from her trip. I wonder if she'll try to take revenge for all the strong men I've thrown her way, give me a taste of my own medicine with something really big or spiked or something. I wonder if I'll be ok. Maybe I don't care. I said we shouldn't change anything in our arrangement other than that and she agreed. I'm glad to have her on my side.

When she left I looked up the schedule at Awaken and I noticed her wedding ring next to the glossy event calendar. Same old Mindy!

DREAM

I WANT TO RECOUNT TWO DREAMS I HAD RECENTLY. IN THE FIRST, I was flying an airplane, Mindy was going skydiving and the instructor was a very rugged young guy, who I'm sure was Australian, though he didn't speak, and there's not any particular way that Australians look to me. I had to keep the plane on course through turbulence and in the midst of it they jumped out together without saying goodbye. I woke up thinking, "alright, I know what that means." I don't read too much into dreams. I think we pretty much reconstruct them in the first minutes after waking. 99% random, full of our anxieties and associations, and in a way that doesn't have any say, ultimately. But then here's the thing, it still casts this kind of spell over us. So even if dreams aren't directly interesting, it's interesting that we can't seem to convince ourselves of that.

It's a little bit like sexual fantasy, or my nature walk feelings about the life inside of life, the protein machine that we're all cogs in. It's a dimension of truth that intersects ours without quite taking us by force. Maybe the only things we know how to call real are the things that force us to acknowledge them. Maybe the dream world is real in its own way, just cucked by the world of cause, necessity, science, by a world that has no compunction about taking you by the scruff and grinding you into the bed. Or the ground. Dreams are more like a smile from across the room. Nervous guy, "yeah, my wife knows I'm here. I'm exploring."

Why do I even remember my dreams? It'd be alright to forget them. Maybe the fact that I hold onto them is related to the way I never really accepted what it is to be a man. I never accepted reality. I was always a cheerleader for another world, that touches this one. But I'm a cheerleader for the brutes too. I'm like a dog, I like everybody. Dreams are a fairy thing, the touch is so light. Is this religion? I feel like what I believe in is nothing like God, it's something right here in a guy like Bill. Maybe that's what Christianity is.

I had another dream where I was looking in the mirror, which it occurs to me now I've never done in a dream. A mirror seems like it's just a little too complicated for the sleeping brain to hold together. And that's how it was here, nothing was wrong exactly, but the details kept shifting in ways that didn't make sense. I was staring at myself in the mirror, but it wasn't myself at all, it was another guy. And then it wasn't a mirror at all but a window, and I wasn't looking out but looking in. So who was this man, in my house, with my wife? I beat on the glass but they heard nothing in the rain and I came around to the front door. Now it wasn't raining, and I was dry.

The house was mine, but it was also a place I hadn't been to for a long time. It seemed to be on an island, overlooking a cliff. There was a typewriter and a stack of papers, a manuscript that seemed unfinished, called "because its light was enough for me." All I remember about it was that it seemed to be in free-hand in spite of the typewriter just there. When you read in a dream there's this explosion of language. I walked off of the balcony and down these wooden platforms and staircases until I was in an ocean lit up like sunset. It occurred to me that I was inside the sunset. There was a ship there and I climbed aboard. I don't remember what happened after that, but I was in the bedroom.

In the bedroom, the man from the mirror or window or whatever was definitely there. I knew it was him, and Mindy too. But they had their backs to me. The room was lit by a single candle, but didn't feel dark. I asked, "what's going to happen?"

This seemed odd as well, in most of my dreams I don't speak, no one does, we're just presence. There's no sound. Mindy replied "I think you already know. You'll see. But you won't see. You'll hear." Then I blew out the candle.

What does it all mean? I ought to ask Clive, he seems to have an answer to everything, though he mostly never shares it. You can talk to him for an hour and think you've learned something, then remember how silent he was, how much "yes" and "say more" there is. This is just like the Carl Rogers thing, but somehow twisted to mean something different.

I don't know what these dreams are but I keep having them, and finally I think the reality of them is something that I belong to, something that I believe in, even if nobody else does, and even if it doesn't hold me at gunpoint like the work-a-day world does.

I don't know why I call it the work-a-day world, I've been living off of my inheritance so long I can hardly remember what work was. I know working people, and I love them, I love Bill. That's why I've been getting into socialism, though I don't see it like they do, as almost a war between guys like Bill and guys like me.

I wish I could set Bill free from his anxiety about money and actually I could do it, but then he wouldn't be Bill. I know what's going to happen, I'm going to give away all of my money and then I'm going to end up alone and poor for the first time in my life in my forties. None of the other poor people are going to like me because I won't know how to act and I won't have struggled. No, I have to go on to the end, I think, exactly as I am, and without disturbing the others.

SATORI

I MET THE MOST MARVELOUS PERSON AT THE MUNCH, PATRICK'S partner Satori. We didn't get much of a chance to talk then, but she told me to stop by Awaken sometime, and I did. Something about her made me brave. I think normally when people make open-ended invitations to me I don't show up, I get lost in thinking about whether I'm showing up too soon, too often. I'm too puppy dog, I should be trying to be cool. Then I am too cool, and they think I don't like them. Or they don't think anything at all. They think "where'd he go?" Then they forget.

I was a little scared that we wouldn't have anything to talk about. She's a little younger than me, a little more counterculture, beautiful dreadlocks. She's probably been to Burning Man. We could talk about Reno! But I don't know anything about tattoos or yoga. As we talked I felt ready to reinvent myself completely if it gave us more of a hook to keep going. Fantasies of full back yakuza tattoos, Darryl the dragon. According to Clive I have an "unstable sense of self." But he's wrong, because an instant later, I saw that I wouldn't have to change at all. I haven't felt this way in a long time, it feels like a true encounter. The kind of thing people call "love at first sight," when they haven't done much introspection. If love was the only kind of deep encounter that you knew how to name or think about, then maybe that's the word you'd have to use. But Satori and I, we're experienced, we're painting with a different palette. We can feel without labels. We don't have to say "love." We've met a few times since our first conversation. I might be in love with her.

Satori and Patrick are so smart about their lifestyle shenanigans. They always seem to know just when to bring it up, and when not to. There are times where you could write Satori off as a "yoga chick" and then you sort of get the depth she has. I wish I could explain the effect. She read my Tarot, because of course she knows about Tarot. I drew the Five of Cups, then the Tower, then the Hanged Man, then we fell apart laughing. She said, "to judge by these cards you're the walking dead, maybe we'd better make the most of time," and then we were in bed, it was as simple as that. She moves so gracefully. I think I'd like to be like her, but that feels superfluous, she's enough. We only need one.

Afterwards, we lay out carelessly, open, barely touching, but somehow I felt absolutely held. That was different, normally I'm a tight cuddler. It made me wonder what I was trying to squeeze out of Mindy or Bill, holding and being held so tight, getting more points of contact, synchronizing my breathing with theirs. Maybe I don't have to strive. I was zoning out on that, staring at the incense holder and castanets hung on the wall, and a Mexican poncho in a large frame. There must be a story there.

Satori is such a perfect woman that she makes a man even out of me. I am a man. But my manhood is like a hothouse flower, not of our climate. Delicate, but real. I feel strong. There's a Bob Dylan song where he says "it takes a woman like your kind to find the man in me." So is "your kind" a slightly hippie goth aesthetic in a spiritually realized poly chick? He probably meant a different kind. I think that's why the song works though, it's nothing to do with types. But the song totally inhabits a moment, the guy singing it doesn't know that yet. I never really liked Bob Dylan, it always felt like he was lecturing me or trying to get me to be a Christian or something, but I heard that song in a movie once, and it made me go back to his stuff.

I don't want to make her out to be an angel either. Satori has a real darkness in her, I think much more than she's said explicitly. Whatever it is, I'd forgive it. She was apparently the proprietress of a brothel in town in the early 2000s. Of course that isn't what they called it, it was all wrapped up in the language of sex and body positivity, but I read between the lines. I think there was some trouble with the law and ultimately some people claimed to have been there for bad reasons. And we talked a little about Brad.

Brad apparently was a part of this world only glancingly, he didn't care much for the feminist culture around it. He seemed to be courting the most dangerous aspects of any place he passed through, and he was always passing through. It seems like there's no one that really claims him, except maybe the guys on that forum.

He liked to tell everybody that he'd started running away to LA when he was barely ten years old, supposedly. Who taught him to do that? It's funny how some people always tell you stories about how tough they are, everything they've seen. Mostly they just reveal a lot of damage. Do I do that? Satori called him a tourist, and said that the girls who were in this thing long term didn't romanticize death at all, they wanted health care and a union and protection from the police, more or less the same things Bill talks about. Everybody's a socialist now, even the hookers. I'm glad all of my friends have such a heart, this is something I would have never thought through on my own. I usually just think of the tragedy of people forced into that kind of work, through slavery, poverty, or just too fucked up to do anything else.

She got very angry when I said that, and said that I saw her as special, said "you've admitted you were wrong about me, so follow through, you're wrong about my sisters, too." I cried like a baby. But she was right. I don't know anything about sex work.

I'm really glad I saw that flash of anger. I noticed that it didn't make me feel defensive, or like she was going to leave me. I just wanted to make it right. Maybe people do "sex work" for their own reasons, and not just the ones who write books about it. I wonder if it's the same with us.

I could probably tell my story in a way that makes me seem like the only enlightened cuck, the only one with ideas about it, the spokesman, the exception that proves the rule. And what's the rule, exactly? That we're all deluded fetishists, repressed homosexuals, that we hate women, that we're racists? I don't know what rotten things the world thinks about us. But I'd hate for someone to get to know me and think I'm the only one of my kind with a brain. I do feel alone sometimes in my life but I can't believe that I'm alone in the world. I'm not. There's even a community of us in Portland, I've talked to some of them online. They say we've always been here. Someone retyped a poem that I got to surprise Oothoon with, Byron's "Beppo." Darryl Cook, culture guy. We should start calling Bill our Cavalier Servente. But he didn't take to the opera stuff, so maybe leave I'll leave it be.

I met someone in that same cuck forum whose wife is a cartoonist. They're trying to explain the lifestyle in a way I wouldn't dare to, to a huge audience of normal people. They're young and straight and sort of have a similar vibe to Satori, only with less counter-cultural resonance and less spirituality. Pretty good advertisement for it if you ask me. Spice up your bedroom life with these vibrators that look like they're from Mars. His and hers pegging kits. Become a cuckold. Watch your wife take yards of dick from an endless succession of surfer guys named Blake and Kenny with identical Puka shell necklaces and short blonde beards.

I'm interested in the hard edge she has about Brad, that she'd call him a tourist like that. The fact is, he died young. He was probably murdered. But people talk about it like it was a suicide, I guess because of all the moments he didn't fight along the way. Maybe the way you'd talk about a skydiver who got thrown out of a plane without a parachute. It's somebody's fault but everybody just agrees to write it off. And by the end everything must have felt very automatic even for him. He was sick, he had no options anymore, he belonged to Clive. Satori and Clive are apparently friends and have intense spiritual discourses. I can't imagine it. Every time I talk to Clive it's "yes?" or "say more?" but somehow Satori will say she talked with him about the difficulty of forgiving themselves. I shouldn't be surprised, everyone can be themselves around Satori. But what does she see in him? And why isn't she scared of him?

I must be wrong about her somehow. It's dangerous to

believe anyone's perfect. And I mean, I don't literally believe that, but my heart basically does. For now I'm just grateful to have this new relationship which is so different than my usual dynamic. When we make love, and it is that, we go very slow, the moment seems to last forever. I've started to think of myself as a bit of a yogi. The other day we held in the moment suspended over orgasm long enough to reflect and I finally saw what all of this has to do with meditation. Then I fell into the void of it. I think that stopping where I was would have been stronger, but instead I let myself be weak, and let the scared desperate animal pound it into her, and cried and was terrified that she would see me in that moment. But she could, and she could forgive me for it, and she didn't even have to forgive me for it. She liked it! I'm still thinking about that. If that animal in me can be loved, and it can, by Satori, doesn't that change everything? I want her to tattoo me. I don't want to forget that.

SLEEPOVER

Since Mindy's still in Northampton, I invited Bill to stay
the night. I didn't exactly invite him to do that, but I invited him
over to watch movies and we got wasted as usual and obviously
he wasn't gonna drive home. Sometimes I wish I could be sober
with him, but that's what it takes with a guy like him. And
besides, I've kind of given up on being sober. I drink with my
friends who drink. I'd probably do G with my friends who do G,
but nobody does G, which is probably a good thing for me. I was
really out of control with that stuff. But I'm not out of control
now. And I was actually shocked by how smoothly it all went
with Bill. I was a little more dressed up than usual and he took it
in stride. I felt like because Mindy and Kit weren't there I could
admit to myself that I felt like a woman with him. And he was
such a man!

After all of my thinking about it and all of my working up to
the thing with toys, Bill actually fucked me and it was, I don't
know, it didn't feel the way I'd hoped but also I felt complete in a
way I hadn't before. Mostly after. During was a little like going to
the dentist. The toys weren't good practice for how he moves,
but none of them were good practice for how motivated I was to
take it. So ups and downs, or maybe ins and outs. I felt myself
moving with him and it all made sense. There were no worries.
What was this like before silicone lube?

I felt how naturally he moved, and I'm glad I felt that, Satori moves that way too, but not as rough. Yin and yang. He spooned me for a while after and I got cleaned up. I'm still thinking about the feeling of him in me, how much it meant to me when he came, how he seemed to be striving to get as far inside as he possibly could at the moment of release, and how he moved then. I wasn't even hard, it was all about him. I was hard after, every time I think about it. And I had this kind of well-fucked feeling that was better than I'd ever imagined it would be. I think women have the better part of sex, and apparently I can play along too.

It actually felt so good that I wondered whether it would work with someone who doesn't know me, and who doesn't have to look past my male body, just a regular gay guy. Luckily I don't have to find out. I have Bill, it feels like I really have him now. But I can see why gay guys all jump into bed with each other so fast, this is great.

In the morning, I asked if he wanted to come with me to the mall and he hesitated. I thought, right, it's weird for you to be seen with me. Especially like this. That feeling of belonging-to-him that I have now, he feels that too. Maybe strangers can feel it. I was frustrated, told him in anger that I love him, that I do everything for him, then paused. "Let me wind that back, ok?" "Ok." It was just a new set of emotions. We talked through it a little. I know Bill is scared of love.

We talked a little about Brad finally and I understood a bit more. Brad had been Bill's younger brother, or half-brother, that much I knew. And he had run away early because he was gay, and maybe more importantly than that, Bill thought something had happened to him as a kid that he never talked to anyone about. He was very sick when he died, so that nobody quite knew what his death meant, or his self-destructive behavior, which started a long time before he got sick. I thought about a documentary I once watched about a guy called Bob Flanagan, who was a masochist and did a lot of very painful performance art because he already had chronic pain from a condition he was dying of. Something in his lungs. I think there was more to it than that, but what do I know about art? I thought ok, maybe Brad was a little bit like that. I asked if he knew about Clive.

"You mean Brian?"

"Yeah. I figure that's the same guy." I didn't want to say too much.

"You figured right. That guy belongs in jail. I might go to jail for kicking his ass if I ever see him."

"Bill, am I safe?"

"I don't know."

SCAB

THINGS WITH SATORI FEEL BETTER THAN EVER. WHEN I'M WITH her, I feel like maybe I could be a well-adjusted poly guy. Bisexual. I never used that word for myself before. Is it possible that's what was going on with me all along? Anything's possible. That's the thing, everything's possible now.

I think I need to be with people who are spiritually realized and direct in a certain way, and that's frightening. It's scary because that's not how I see Mindy, or Bill. Especially Mindy, it feels like I don't know her sometimes. But here's an observation: I have this endlessly elaborate interior monologue, right? I feel like I'm always narrating. But everyone I love is full of silence. Whether that's Clive's coldness, Bill's inarticulate masculinity, Satori's oceanic depths. So where's my silent place? Or are they all chattering to themselves inwardly just like I am? Maybe from the outside, I look like them, and this is just the view from the inside that everybody has. But I don't think so. I think that silence is a real place, and I think Satori helps me find it.

After I came this morning I lay there in this quiet moment that felt like forever. I wasn't male or female, there wasn't success or failure, there wasn't even the absence of those things. It was just a moment unmoored from striving, thinking, speaking, not even talking to myself. I don't need to label it. I wondered after whether this wasn't what orgasms were supposed to be like, like, maybe the simplicity of other people, and the way they chase it, it's because this feeling is more accessible to them. I'm always saying that, everybody else is simpler than me. I thought about Bill speeding up at the end, in the heat of it, chasing something that isn't there. He can't get me pregnant. I wish he could.

Mindy got back a couple days ago and seems to mostly approve of what's been going on, but she's a little bit off doing her own thing. She had a session with Clive and it ended up injuring her pretty badly. She says he wasn't trying to do it, and I believe that, he's just too thick. But that's pretty cold comfort considering what else he's done when he wasn't trying to. Is that how he killed Brad? Hopefully she can just rest up and it'll get better, but she's not having sex for a few weeks. And Kit, who'd seemed for her part so romantic, seems angry. I think this is part of the lesbian thing, ultimately there's a bit of a rage that she isn't enough for Mindy, and that women in general aren't. I think bisexual women must have a hard time with that kind of thing. But I sympathize with the lesbian side of it too, like, wouldn't you want to know someone didn't see you as a phase, or as a little something on the side of their real relationship, or their real life? I can see Kit's side of things. But that's not Mindy, she's just tired and a little sore. I get that too. Satori gave me some jojoba oil and told me how to use it, I hope it helps. I'm gonna take an epsom salt bath too.

It's funny, as excited as I was before about Mindy using a strap-on, or Satori, I don't really want that. I can't even imagine asking Satori for that, even though I know she'd take it in stride. I want to be penetrated, and I'm getting that from Bill. That's something I want from men who are men. I don't mince around. I wonder what Oothoon's deal is with that, what kind of expectations people bring to her about it. Half of me wants to start a conversation to ask, but I think that must be another thing that gets old if you're trans, people asking lurid questions about your dick under the cover of being an ally. "Does that feel strange? Do people treat you badly? Do you wish it wasn't there?" She says she wants to talk about poetry and I'm happy to do that although I don't always feel like I can keep up. And actually, when I talked about poems I knew like Byron or Walt Whitman, she didn't have that much to say. But she talks about trans stuff all the time, maybe next time she does I'll sneak the question in there. I can be slick.

Satori had to cut our session pretty short because she's meeting up with another lover. I can't stand this guy, a young "relationship anarchist" guy with a lotus tattoo on his neck. He's a yoga instructor, a kundalini something-or-other, and an "energy practitioner." Sometimes I think I've got to get out of this town, it's full of hippies. Reno's got its own problems but at least people there don't claim to be arhats. And now here's this guy who at the age of 28 is passing himself off as an enlightened spiritual teacher. And you know what? He might be. What kind of a guy calls himself Moonbeam? Well, what kind of a guy puts on a little dress and begs his best friend to fuck him and to fuck his wife? It's not like I can judge exactly, but there's something about guys like Moonbeam that gets under my skin. Like it's all love and light with them. I sort of wonder if we're the same species.

To me a guy that acts that way is a scab. That's a word I learned from Bill, for a working man who betrays the union. It reminds me of school, of the people who were so chipper and did their homework a week in advance, who got up early, the shiny-apple-for-teacher guys. I'd always think, "don't you see how much harder that makes it for the rest of us? Don't you see that you're trading on our misery?" Fuck you, Moonbeam. You don't know what it's like. I look into his eyes and all I see is a world where I have to be like him to be worthy of love, that's all I can think about. It's a world where I'm wrong, and where I'm worthless. And it's just a different brain chemistry that gives him that. When Clive gave me MDMA I was like Moonbeam for exactly three hours. Then I was down for a week. He's like that all the time and apparently the better part of this world, which is Satori, belongs to guys like that. Why? Another inch? Serotonin? Oxytocin?

Breathe, Darryl. Breathe. This is jealousy. Why isn't it hot?

INJURY

CLIVE CANCELLED ON ME! JUST AS WELL THAT HE DID, I'M STILL sore from Bill, I don't think hiking would be very fun right now. I think my curiosity about him has really diminished since making so much progress with Satori and Mindy and Bill. It's like it was all a dream, all of that darkness. It's bad enough that he killed Brad, it's bad enough that he ruined my wife with his big stupid cock, I'm ready to not think about him for a little while. I wonder if he's embarrassed. He once told me that he doesn't know how to apologize to people, he just goes away for a long time and lets them process it, then he returns a few times. If they don't want to forgive and forget, he's gone. Wasn't there something about vampires not going in where they're not invited?

I'm sure we'll see him again. Meanwhile I've built up a serious supply of psychedelics from him, I might take some again soon. He must know that I'm doing this, I buy them every chance I get but I don't take them very often. So I've got a freezer full. I'm overdue for it, I think. I've been thinking about it, it's so different than the GHB I used to take all the time. Tripping isn't about fuzzing out or taking me out of it at all, and it isn't even about feeling good. If anything, it's a way to feel more intensely. That's what I want, now. I wonder if Satori would want to do it with me.

I've been writing more to Oothoon, and it occurs to me that I never say her real name. It's Jenny, I always think of her as "Oothoon" because she introduced herself to us under her pen name when we met on that road trip. I miss those moments and I think I might go out to see her soon. She invited me to stay with her for a bit "next time I'm in Reno" and I thought, you know, why not? I could visit my mom, that could be an excuse. But I don't want to leave Eugene until Mindy's feeling better, and that might be a bit. I can't imagine what it's going to be like with Oothoon. Are we going to have sex? What does she see in me? Is she trying to "recruit" me? Maybe it doesn't matter. Satori told me that I should be saying "Yes to Life" and that sounded so right until she added the context that it was something Moonbeam had said about me. That burns me up. I don't want to believe they talk about me, all I want is peace from that guy. All he wants is peace too, everybody acting his way, all smoothed out. I think I've never hated a guy more than that, not even Greg.

When we met Oothoon, she was in our world. We were on a road trip, we were playing pool, and here was this tranny in our group. She actually walked up to us, tweaked the flower behind my ear, mine was on the left, Mindy's was on the right. She asked "so which is which, swingers?" and picked up a flower from the tables, put it in her teeth and sunk the eight ball. It didn't strike me as particularly female, but God was it cool. I guess I shouldn't say "tranny," but she used it for herself. She makes a lot of jokes. But when I go there, I'm going to be at her house, with all of her roommates and her friends and all of her books on the shelf. I've got to be careful. Somehow I never thought to imagine what her life is like. She wasn't always in Reno, she told me she was living in San Francisco when she transitioned, and maybe New York too? Her stories always sound so amazing and impossible, full of amazing and impossible people. I wonder what that's like though, to transition someplace full of people just like you, full of all the freaks and weirdos, and then to just move out to the middle of nowhere. Well, Reno isn't nowhere, but you know what I mean.

MOONBEAM

I HAD TEA, BECAUSE OF COURSE IT WOULD BE TEA, WITH SATORI
and Moonbeam. I want to die. There's a way of moving that
these yoga guys have, I just hate it. I don't know what makes it
different than Satori's way of moving, her "presence," but it is.
Why does he breathe so slowly? It's as though he has to wear his
progress in meditation all the time like peacock feathers. I
thought the whole point of meditation was that it isn't about
that, but here we are. Another thing for me to be worse at. It's
bad enough that I'm older, that I'm in worse shape, that he probably has a better dick than me. I don't want to think about that.

I don't know why it was so easy to cope with all the other
guys when it was Mindy, even in the first stages of our lifestyle
exploration. I think the difference is that I'm over it, I really am
just over being a cuck. But now here comes Moonbeam, the
punishing reminder that being a cuck isn't a matter of an
enlightened lifestyle at all, it was never a choice, never a kink, it
was just a fact. It's a fact about nature and it's confirmed in the
heart. He's the better man, so he'll take my woman. They
always do.

What I feel for Satori is so pure and I haven't felt that before.
It's a different kind of love. I think I get better and better at
falling in love in my life, there was Mindy, then Bill, and now
Satori. And I do feel very modern in one way: I feel like I can

love them all, I really do. I'm full of warm feelings for Oothoon, for Patrick, even for Clive. Why not? But just now when I finally have something like a normal sexual connection with Satori, I can see it already. She's going to leave me. That'll be it. That's her prerogative. She'll pick up her ball and go home. She'll find someone more fun to play with. I don't know what I'll do.

I reached for the teapot and they both laughed, I guess at the idea I'd be so impatient, direct, impolite, un-Japanese. "Hold on, Darryl, we've got time." Moonbeam poured me a cup in what looked like slow motion, from a great height, and painted a Japanese character on a scroll. "Calligraphy," he said, in a very satisfied way. I almost laughed. Of course it's calligraphy, that's literally the fucking word for the thing that you're doing right now. Do you have anything to say about it? I think Moonbeam never has anything to say about anything, but he has this way of speaking that clearly conveys at least that that he thinks he did, that he's communicated something very deep, and we're all supposed to appreciate it. We're all supposed to just play along. And now I have to. I can't say how annoyed I am, because I have to convince Satori that I'm on the level, that I'm a spiritual guy too. Unless they're testing me. Are they testing me?

When I finally took a sip of the tea, and seemed to drain the tiny cup much too fast, Moonbeam poured me another, this time from even higher, and drew another character, definitely different than the first one. That made me wonder if he even knew what he was writing. It's not like we'd know, maybe they're just squiggles. He looked into the middle distance and asked, "Darryl, you seem to be a man who thinks. What do you think about the nature of time and the moment called now?"

What a question! How can anyone think anything about time, it's so abstract and confusing. But these people romanticize it. They like the confusion. I tried to say something too literal, that subjective time is sort of false, that what appears to be a sequence of moments isn't that at all. I said that when we think we're being, we're really remembering, what gets called experience is something assembled in retrospect, and that there are really no true moments. Satori and Moonbeam both stared for a while and Satori asked if I really thought that, that there is no moment. The look in her eyes was sort of sad, the way Christians look at you when they realize you're not just another prodigal son, that you actually don't believe in their guy and you're going to hell for that reason.

I wondered if I wasn't missing something, I don't know. Like I was supposed to say "Be Here Now?" That's the magic phrase, right? But I was frustrated and said yes, and that I wasn't taken in by the new age cult of immediacy and presence, and I tried to explain what I'd been talking about with Oothoon, that spiritual people seem to just be privileging a special layer of experience, the one that feels "primordial." The layer that appears as what's given, as what's under, or what's before. That's just a part. It's the bottom part. Does that make any sense at all? Satori and Moonbeam seemed sure that it didn't. Satori actually seemed hurt, and Moonbeam seemed amused. That's two strikes. Then Moonbeam said that he thought that there is such a thing as now and that he could prove it to me right here. As horrifying as that sounded to me, it was a very aggressive thing for him to say, a bit out of his usual mode, which made me feel a little smug, just knowing that he's on his back foot. I agreed.

He asked me to sit cross-legged and when I told him I'd be too uncomfortable he offered that I could sit on my knees. He supplied a cushion and down to the floor I went. He said "we ought to breathe together" and began to outline a spiritual exercise. I don't like this kind of thing. I especially don't like how he had me off guard, like not only did he know everything that was going to happen, doing anything besides following his orders always seems to mean being not fun enough, or not spiritual enough, or not present enough, or not saying a clear enough Yes to Life and to the moment, and everything else. So I have to do everything Moonbeam tells me. Why don't you just put it in my mouth you hippie bastard? Why can't I just blow you? Why do you have to humiliate me like this? But I had to stay focused as he explained the exercise.

What he suggested was similar to a very basic form of mindfulness meditation that I actually do. Ok. He said I should breathe calmly and that we should look at each other, not intently at any given part of the body, and not to look at or think about anything else. It's just taking one another's body as an object of meditation, and he said that we could do it for ten minutes. He produced a drum and a large hourglass from his seemingly endless bag and asked Satori to strike it once to begin the meditation and twenty-one times to end it. I asked why twenty-one and immediately regretted asking. "The Major Arcana, Darryl. We begin with the Magician, and end with the World." He says my name too often, I don't know why people do that.

"I thought the first card was the Fool?" I asked, thinking I was getting one over.

"That's zero, Darryl, at the beginning and the end. That's us." Fucking Moonbeam. He cast a glance to Satori, but I couldn't make eye contact. She was looking at Moonbeam. We began the exercise.

I was ready for this, I've actually meditated plenty, though I never imagined as I was doing it that I was preparing myself for war. Am I fighting this angel-headed devil for Satori's heart? That isn't right, Satori isn't someone who can be won. She has her own agency. So why am I worried about Moonbeam taking — BANG!

Breathe.

This reminds me a little of my cuckolding scenes with Mindy, it just feels like a game. I mean, I wouldn't have said that was a game at the time, but now it all feels so silly. Maybe we "play" after all. Moonbeam must be insecure too or he wouldn't toy with me like this. Unless he's cruel. But he's not like Clive. Look at him.

Breathe.

Cuckolding was never about Mindy, and I wonder if that hurts her. Does she go along with it because it's the only way I can love her? Can I love her? I think I don't.

Breathe.

Whatever this game is, it isn't about Satori either. I thought I would disappoint her by failing to play along, but now I think I've disappointed her by locking spiritual horns. All I want to do is to cry out to her, like I cried the other day during sex, that I love her and I don't want to do this, and that I'll just see her tomorrow. I don't care that she fucks him. He isn't the only one she fucks, I never needed that, I just want to feel like she won't leave me, and that they won't laugh at me. That I'm not broken and alone.

Breathe.

Back to the situation, Moonbeam's hair is just a little bit wavy, dark brown and his eyes are very green. If he grew a mustache he'd look like Yanni. His face is simultaneously frozen and relaxed in the way experienced meditators are, presumably after staring in the mirror for a long time. It's just social conformity but to a group that cuts across time. There's a simpler word for that. It's an aesthetic.

Breathe.

Very open now, peaceful. I feel the way Moonbeam must want me to feel, I guess. Moonbeam is the master. Very aware of all of the light flooding in through the skylight in the studio and no idea how long it's been. Seeing the light like honey, pouring in, flooding, letting the level rise up to my neck. And a little past? Feeling my chin, thinking about the stubble there, I hate it. Moonbeam has a little beard and the hair looks soft. Good genes? Expensive conditioner? Probably both. I'm not counting my breaths or counting time. Should I be counting? This was a beautiful feeling but it spun out so fast into questions, try again.

Breathe.

In complete harmony now. Moonbeam is powerful, but I'm powerful in my own way, just less of the warrior. I'm neutral being, and I flow like honey. Like water. If I didn't have my stories, and my situation, I'd still be that. Everything is that, and it has a flavor.

Breathe.

So that's Being. Watching it divide again into self and world, inside and outside, but seeing both sides yawning empty. I'm this membrane between them which seems to warp and vibrate, stretched like the skin of a drum. Or maybe I'm a tiny droplet of water that condenses on the membrane for a moment, refracts the brilliant ceiling light, and then the mallet sends us spinning. Or it never comes and we evaporate. Or we're surrounded by other little drops, all condensing here until we merge. Drip! But the drop is on the inside. That's the difference between me and him.

Breathe.

I have to pull myself together, but I can't let him see me pulling myself together. I can't even let him see me freeze and reflect on how to pull myself together. Nothing is imperceptible here. I just have to let myself come back from whatever that was and stay focused on him. What is he doing over there? What is he seeing right now? Was he on the other side of the skin?

Breathe.

Did Moonbeam turn me into a bright light in a droplet of water on the tight skin of a drum? Am I losing my mind? What the fuck does this have to do with "the moment?" I feel just as narrativized as I ever was, those experiences were still experiences, so they had packed into them this feeling of recollection, like always. I was imagining what it would be like to recount that moment, what it would be like to remember it and be haunted by it. And probably I was inventing it after the fact.

Can't breathe. BANGING.

I don't know what happened to all of the time, obviously the action that transpires in ten minutes meditation could fill a book if you really paid attention. Mostly you just let go of it. It's much like dreams that way, an order of reality that doesn't hold us at gunpoint and demand to be honored. We're allowed to forget about it, and given all of the other important things we have to remember, maybe we should. Maybe its lack of necessity and purpose is what connects it to beauty. But this time, I had to remember, there was something on the line. Moonbeam, once again totally assured that he had communicated something, asked or said "see?" Certainly his voice was inquisitive, but the question seemed rhetorical.

I was speechless, and just said that I would like to bow to him. Then I asked Satori for a long hug and made to leave. Moonbeam giggled a little and asked if I wouldn't like to hug him too. Sure. There's no possible limit to humiliation. He held me in his strong hands, which reminded me of Bill's hands, I didn't expect that. He held me with his big open smile that seemed to mock me, as if to say, "that wasn't hard for me, Darryl.

I have no hangups, Darryl. I have no hangups and I'm going to take everything you love away from you and everything that you are. You're just a little drop of water, Darryl. I'm the light." When I broke from his arms I turned to Satori but she'd already turned away. I didn't want to beg her for more attention after I'd already said goodbye so I quickly shuffled out the door. I heard her shout "bye, Darryl!" as I ran out the door and I shouted back, "see you soon I hope!" which seemed like a nonchalant and not very needy thing to say, but my voice cracked a little. There was nothing to do but begin to run and I did. I gave up after about half a mile. Then I was panting and walked the rest of the way. I stopped at a Starbucks, I need real coffee. Moonbeam runs marathons. I wish I was dead.

DAMN COFFEE

WHEN I ARRIVED HOME I THINK MINDY WANTED TO TALK TO ME, but I said that I couldn't, that I needed to decompress. I felt bad about that, but it was true. I've been thinking a little about why we even live out here in Eugene. I came here for college, met Mindy, we had a kid, and it's just felt like we were stuck here, even though we can go anywhere now. Especially now that Tony's out of the house. It's been a few years of freedom now, and the only thing new is the lifestyle. We could have never done that while he was at home. But maybe we should be thinking bigger.

We visited my mom on our Winter trip to Nevada and I guess I'm going to see her again next time I go. That's why I'll say I'm going, but I'm really going to visit Oothoon. I wonder how my mom's doing, we haven't talked all that much since I tried to "come out" as a cuckold. I mean, we talk but the conversations haven't felt real. I think she always saw me as a loser. I can't even imagine what she must think now. And there's the problem of a mother's intuition. She'd be able to sense the subtle changes, how smooth I am, how I've let the edge go out of my voice, all that growl and affected baritone just gone. I think I'll have to stay away for a little while longer.

You know how it goes when you say you want to be alone and then immediately you find yourself wanting to call a friend, or you waste time online? I couldn't contain myself. I paged Clive and to my surprise he called back right away. He said we may as well meet for coffee this time, he just won't have any. I won't either, I just had some. But that's fine. I told Mindy about the change of plans, jumped into the shower and went to meet him. When the hot water hit my neck I was gone again, but it wasn't comforting, I just thought about Moonbeam and the water drops. Same Starbucks.

Clive says he likes Starbucks because it's faceless. That suits him, the anonymity of it. I sort of think he likes it because none of the locals go there, and you never see the same people working there. It's always someone new, someone young. Even the managers, it seems like they could be printing new people in a lab every morning, or flying them in. Going there means you're from California or something, or maybe LA. Soulless. For a guy like Clive, who's avoiding a lot of people, and maybe hasn't got a soul, that sounds pretty perfect. What's he even doing here? It struck me last night that Clive makes more sense as an LA guy, although what do I know about LA? I sometimes think I can't really see Clive because I just see this swirl of media about guys like him, which is all designed to make him look scary. He is scary. Underneath all of that illusion is a real coldness and you come to know it if you look into his eyes.

I asked him what had originally got him interested in psychology, and he said that people had studied him as a child. He sort of wanted to turn the lens back on them, and to have their tools. "Besides," he said, "to quote Paul Valéry, 'a man should go into himself armed to the teeth.'" Very pithy, very cultured guy. I wonder what that sounds like in French, I'm sure he could tell me. And I wonder how all of these people have so much reading behind them. I have all the time in the world to do it but it somehow just never happens. I told him I was reading John Berryman and he just laughed, said that was appropriate. Then I told him about Oothoon.

"Clive, am I a transsexual in denial?"

"On this occasion I will venture a bit of directness, Darryl: certainly not. But—" He seemed to trail off. So we left the conversation there. He really is Hannibal Lecter. But we agree on that, I'm not.

I suggested we talk about something else and finally got the nerve to ask him about Brad. He sort of paused and asked me how much I knew. I said I knew that Brad had been very sick, that I'd seen the forum and wondered if he was the guy that people there called Brian, but that I thought a lot of what was written there was probably lies.

"They are lies."

"But something happened."

"Yes."

"And he's dead. Brad, I mean. He was a real person. There's a video."

"Yes."

It didn't feel safe to ask more. I wanted to ask him how he got away with it. I don't know why I wasn't more frightened, but it somehow felt alright. We're ok. I'd never knowingly spoken with a killer until then, but Clive is just Clive. I'm certain he's dangerous to someone, but I think it's safe for me. Nobody understands that, and I sometimes think that's why the world is such a mess. You want to imagine that it's a totally different kind of person that causes all the trouble, that you can get rid of him and your problems will go away. It's especially tempting to try to get rid of someone like Clive because he really is different. But violence doesn't come from people, it comes from situations. They do it because they can, and because they get carried away. I don't think Clive can hurt me, of course we can all hurt each other, he hurt Mindy just the other day. But I don't think my vulnerability really matches his excess, for the most part. I'm not his perfect victim. So we can be friends. He said a big part of his therapy was learning to think ahead about situations where he'd want to hurt people and where he'd be able to, and trying to avoid them. Said he tries to keep himself accountable by checking in with Derek, who's like him. Buddy system, I guess.

I asked if that meant the BDSM lifestyle and he said that was it, more or less. I had to wonder about that. I also had to wonder whether his game of being a hypnotist and a drug dealer and an alpha in the cuckolding lifestyle wasn't actually kind of the same situation he was supposed to be avoiding. But it is different. I can really see that with Patrick and Satori. There's a feeling in the lifestyle of being in an underworld, but it's usually pretty tooth-less. Bumper bowling feeling. It's only dangerous when the guard rails fail. That's Clive. I sort of think with him that we're dealing with something much more absolute, and it's at once a lot scarier and something that makes more sense to me. I'd take Clive over Moonbeam any day, and I told him that.

Clive sort of chuckled when I mentioned Moonbeam and I asked if they knew each other. Apparently they did, through martial arts. This town is too small. I felt a little guilty about it but I asked if Clive would beat up Moonbeam a little on my behalf, next time they sparred. I asked if he could hurt him a little. For me. Clive said, "think carefully about this, Darryl. You know that if you ask me to do this, I will."

"Ok. Make it hurt."

GAMES WITH BILL

THINGS ARE LOOKING UP. MINDY'S FEELING MOSTLY BETTER AND I booked a flight to Reno after all, rented a car there. I got a pretty nice one, but not too nice, because I figured that might set something off with Oothoon and her friends. I was complaining that you can't bring lube through the airport anymore and Mindy laughed a little. She reached into her purse and produced a travel bottle, Kit found it before their big trip to Northampton. Better living through chemistry! I'm going to stay with Oothoon for three days, then visit my mom, then fly back home that night. I'm ready to step out of my world, away from the hippies and the killers and even from Bill, though we had a great time last night.

I'm surprised that having real sex turns out to have been a rare thing and a little sad about it, but I think I might be more into the fantasy than the reality of anal. That's not right, in a way I feel like I want it all the time, but all the energy of preparing for it and feeling clean enough to do it is too much. I guess this is what experience is for. But for now it just feels like too much of a hassle compared to blowing him, which is 90% of what we do. Again, always, we're drunk, though this time I pushed him a little. I think I've convinced him to take some of Clive's pills with me, which should be really interesting. Before we got into drinking I asked him to play Moonbeam's game with me, just looking at each other for a few minutes. Ten is actually way too much, though.

I don't know how to explain how it was, certainly it wasn't as deep as the experience with Moonbeam, we're both not such magical people. Bill squirmed more than I expected, I think he isn't used to being seen. That was most of what I saw, I thought, you know, if you're walking down the street nobody sees you for very long, nobody hears you. And even when you're together with someone, you don't really look. Is it for a reason? I can't tell if we're starved for this kind of face communion or if we've organized our world to eliminate it for a good reason. Maybe it just hurts. Either way, there's no normal way in Bill's life for people to look at him for an extended period of time, unless he's at the doctor, or maybe in sex. But in sex, it's all wild abandon, and he likes to take us face down anyway. I like that too. I think of face to face sex as kind of like sixty-nine, a compromise for no one in particular. Who has time for that much feminism? Or it isn't even, you know, it's just attachment to an idea of equality of effort, or equality of focus. I hate that. Just fuck me hard and get your rocks off. If I'm on my knees, I'm serving you. It's about you. You can do something for me later, but even then it shouldn't be in a spirit of exchange, never because you feel like you should. I don't think it's the mark of a caring lover to be hung up on equality like that. Just fuck me into the bed and have the decency not to ask me, "was it good for you?" It was, by defini-tion. I felt this kind of motion in me and surprisingly, started to have more of an erection, which Bill noticed.

He asked to touch me. Breaking from the game he started to stroke through my clothes and it felt good, not as good as Satori, and he even kissed me, which he'd never done before. The feeling of his stubble against my smooth face is something I won't forget for a long time. Maybe face to face is alright after all? But in a short time he broke from the embrace. "I think I'm not gay, Darryl, I'm sorry. I can't do this."

"You don't have to."

He gave me a long hug and I asked if the hand stuff before had been ok. It was. I said I didn't need him to push past any new boundaries, everything we'd done before was enough for me. I just want more of it. I think messing around with these Moonbeam games sort of destabilized us and I wondered why I thought it would be a good idea to try, what I was even looking for there. Is meditation just a wily road to intimacy? We drank a lot and dissolved the mood in guy stories. He's good at that, he can always break a mood. I wondered if it wasn't similar to his face, nobody looks at him for long, and in conversations it's the same. Bill doesn't want to get to the bottom of things. And I don't really need him to. But there's something in himself that he's so scared of.

I sometimes think I ought to be more frightened. Frightened of myself and of everybody else. I don't even mean just Clive. I think I have this prejudice that every rock is worth turning over. That's not how it should be. Like, at any given moment in our life, part of ourselves is submerged and part is not. It's easy to reach for whatever seems deepest, but when we grasp it we find we've only turned over, like a boat capsizing again and again. Are we supposed to spin forever? How to pump it out? I don't think the metaphor goes that far. Oothoon called me an "introspective voyager," and it stuck with me. It's from a poem called "The Comedian as the Letter C." I shot back "is the C for cuckold? See you soon. Sincerely, Darryl." and wondered if it wasn't weird to send an email at two in the morning. Actually the email I wrote was really long, I talked about everything, but I still didn't mention Clive. Just flipping rocks until they spin.

RENO

RENO'S REALLY CHANGED SINCE I LEFT FOR COLLEGE, A LITTLE early in 1989. At some point in the nineties I mostly stopped visiting, and my parents moved to Sparks. I said it was because of the memories of my dad but really I just didn't care for the place. As soon as I saw something different I knew I didn't belong there. When I see my mom we make a vacation of it, meeting halfway somewhere, or she comes to the house in Eugene, which has the added advantage of being able to visit her sister. But in the nineties there was nothing there. The second best gambling town with the second best whorehouses — does that sound like a good thing to anybody? Until our road trip I hadn't been back for about a decade, and it had always seemed important to me that I'd left my hometown for good when I went away to college. It reminded me of the stories of Abraham in the bible, I liked that. Now I feel like Abraham again, leaping into the fiery furnace.

I ended up renting a car and a hotel room, in spite of Oothoon's offer to stay at her trans house. I didn't want to step off of the plane straight into her world. I knew I'd want to regroup. She's too young for me. Oothoon might be 35 but she lives the way my friends were living at 22, at least the ones who didn't have kids. Big dilapidated house, two hundred dollar rooms, and God knows who lives there. That's what it sounds like from the emails but maybe it's all a fantasy. I think at least they all have jobs now, and Reno isn't as sad a place as I remember it. People work in technology now, and it's on the corridor for Burning Man, which I think brings a lot of counter-cultural life. Oothoon laughed when I mentioned Burning Man and I'm not sure why, I guess I'll have to ask about it. I was never really a party person, and I always preferred the forest to the desert, so I know why I wouldn't fit in there. But I feel like someone like Ooothoon would really clean up. Maybe she just doesn't need to. Maybe it's corny now.

So I'm full of nervous energy, like, why the hell did I come out here? Why did I tell Oothoon I'd help pay for her surgery? I wonder if I can get out of that. I sometimes have this magnetic curiosity about transsexuals but I think it's faded as things changed with Bill, and especially with Satori. I feel like when I first conceived of this trip I'd just started talking to Oothoon, so everything was new, everything was unsettled. We flipped a rock. Now I'm just following through. Fighting a feeling that I've just grown out of all of it: the cuckolding, the trans connection. I care about love. And I have love. At home.

Here I am on what seems to be a fantastic adventure and all I can think is that I'm already finished, I'm ready to go back. Satori showed me how to be a man with a woman, and Bill showed me how to be a woman with a man or maybe a man with a man, or however you want to label it. And Mindy's there through it all to level me out. That's all I need. When I'm with Satori I think that maybe all of this is just sick, and that maybe I am. Actually it's the furthest thing from my mind in the moments when we're together, but why can't my life just be about something like that? I think I might have to learn to pray.

But of course that world doesn't belong to me. It's some kind of error that I'm even there. Like, how did I meet Satori? Essentially by investigating a murder. What did I think I would find? Not love. But of course I'm sniffing around where I don't belong. I always am. That world belongs to guys like Moonbeam. My wife and I belong to Bill and Clive. And somehow I've taken myself very far away, all the way to Reno, to be taken under the wing of a transsexual poet who thinks she's got the keys to my soul and she's recruiting. Well, at least it's a vacation.

I feel a fear as though Oothoon is going to eat me, and not from hunger. The way you'd eat a bag of chips, you just keep going. It becomes an automatic movement: you don't want it, you don't not want it. Maybe she doesn't care about me at all but I fit her profile for a new recruit to the trans army, and she's going to try to convince me to be like her, damn the consequences in my life.

That or she's really my friend. It's hard to believe. I don't think I'm that interesting, I don't know about books or life or anything. I have a perspective that spins out sometimes and I always think that matters, but uncomfortably. There's a little bit of wisdom in me, but it doesn't belong to me, and I don't know what to do with it.

Oh, right. She's after my money. Maybe I ought to give it to her.

BREAKFAST

WOKE UP THINKING, "WHAT THE HELL AM I DOING IN RENO?" I
feel almost as though I'm in a dream. Sometimes my life feels
like it's too plastic, too free, it isn't relatable to anybody. That's
basically because of my inheritance. Everybody else is making
some kind of plan, because they have to. But I never had to be
good at anything, I never had to be somebody, I was going to be
ok. So maybe I never had to be a man, that's just slack. Maybe I
never had to be a father, not really. Are guys like me the product
of decadence? Certainly of luxury, but I was never so sure what
"decadence" means. It sounds bad.

I sat in the worst, brightest diner I've ever seen this morning
and poked at a plate of eggs for an hour before giving up. The
waitress was even uglier than the girl from the hamburger stand,
but looked like she might have been beautiful once. Too much
makeup. I headed back to the car, to meet Oothoon and her
friend. I wish it wasn't like that, meeting her friends at the same
time as her. But it'll be fine. I'll bet the friend has purple hair
and reads Tarot. Like a female Moonbeam. Or sort of female.

At the diner I was thinking more about Clive, and that a lot
of the behavior we associate with psychopaths is really a rage
and terror at being seen. There's such a thing as impulsive
cruelty, real failures of empathy, but for the most part I think
that's probably episodic and minor. Maybe it's major if you're on

the wrong end of it. But there's a whole personality built around hiding it, controlling or eliminating anyone who might be a witness, or anyone who might threaten your poise. What's different about Clive is that he does allow himself to be seen, and I think that must be very hard to do.

Oothoon had a phrase that resonated for me, "the colder parts of me can be loved," that was from one of her poems. I think Clive is someone who's managed to say that. Except I don't think he needs to be loved, I have to say it that way to relate to him, but I think in the end I can't relate to him. He doesn't have that anxiety about being loved. Love is useless to him.

I don't know what I'm doing running after Clive and I don't know what I'm doing in Reno. Did I come here to transition? I'm not going to transition. Some part of me might have been planning that a few months ago, but I know I'm not trans. I'm probably going to meet Oothoon again in person and this time I'll be sober and pathetic and sweating through my t-shirt and looking like her dad even though I'm only a decade older.

The smartest thing for me to do would be to call Oothoon and say I give up, and that I'm going home. The smartest thing I could do would be to forget about Clive, tell him I don't want to see him again. I think they'd both understand. Oothoon would think I was a coward or afraid to face her level of need. Clive would very carefully disappear from my world, and probably from the world of everybody who knows me, that's what it looks like he did with the Eugene people who knew Brad. You don't beat a murder charge by being reckless.

I'm beginning to like the idea, I could just go back to Eugene right now, tell Mindy that I want to try again. She's not having sex with anyone right now and things are rocky with Kit. The situation with Satori seems alright and seems to have taught me something about being a man. I'm going to call her later. Maybe I'm ok. I'm ok, but somehow I'm here. It's 11:30 and we're meeting at one. I think I might take a drive through Sparks.

SPARKS

Driving through Sparks feels remarkably unremarkable, I could be anywhere. All I feel is anxiety about Oothoon and her friend with the even weirder name. I made a point to do a loop around my old high school. I saw some kids with Railroaders jerseys and wondered if they saw me looking. Probably I looked like a creep to them. These boys are so muscular already in high school, it's the strangest thing. It reminds me a little of how it was when my son was that age, and it reminds me a little of Bill. I think if I got out of the car they'd beat me up and call me a pedophile, or they'd say I was gay. Maybe I am, gay I mean. But I'm not interested. Teenagers make everything about themselves. I can't imagine how it is for Oothoon, like, I can just dress down a little and I'm ok. But I don't think she's ever safe at all around teenage boys. What is it that makes them so cruel?

I thought being near the high school would bring back memories, but it really didn't. That time in my life just doesn't matter. It feels like it's supposed to, but I'm over it. I was over it at the time. Of course it was uncomfortable, everybody was uncomfortable then, but what does it matter? I wasn't too bullied, I had some friends. I even had girlfriends. Mostly I'd run home from school and jerk off. I was waiting for adolescence to end, and it did. I kept my nerve. Then I went to college out of state. I used to have a talent for keeping my head down, I wonder what happened to that. These days it feels like there's an urgency to my life, like maybe this is what a mid-life crisis is. I'm having all of the adventures now that I should have been having when I was 19. Instead I was pretending to be asleep in a bunk bed, staring at the ceiling, wishing I could be her.

What kind of adventure is this though? Watching strangers fuck my wife? Getting feminized? Hanging out with some psycho drug dealer who makes snuff films? The only sweetness and light in my life is a wife who doesn't trust me and a hippie magic mama that's got probably ten guys like me all on a string that she thinks of as therapy cases and sex work clients. I don't know if adventure is really the word for what's happening anymore. I've got to get it under control. There's a feeling of an undertow, and of being far from shore. I don't know, is my life this way because I want it to be? Is there something I'm supposed to be learning from it?

Somehow I'm going to drive over to meet Oothoon at her house in half an hour and I've got to put all these questions out of mind. I said I was coming to town to visit my mom, but my mom actually doesn't know I'm here. I keep getting scared that I'll run into her in Sparks. Maybe I'll get in a car accident or get beaten up by teenagers and that's how she'll find out I was here. But I just didn't want Oothoon to think I was flying to Reno just to visit her. That'd be crazy. Real people don't do that, they have lives that they have to get back to. I think Oothoon has a life too, though I don't totally get it. She's always thinking about poetry, but she doesn't seem attached to anything. I don't see her publishing much of it and I can't imagine it pays. How do people do that? I don't think she's rich.

Why do I feel so blank and dead, when I'm here where it all started? It's like I'm ascending the scaffold, having already said my goodbyes, like I've smoked my last delicious cigarette. I don't even smoke. I don't need to do it again. The past doesn't matter. I'm going to go meet Oothoon and somehow act like a normal person. But I guess not too normal, she's a poet, she digs for the weird. Everything is impossible.

It'll be fine. I tried calling Mindy but she didn't pick up. That's fine too. Mostly I was just glad that she'd see me on the caller ID. We keep up appearances for each other like that.

TRANS HOUSE

WHAT CAN I SAY ABOUT OOTHOON'S HOUSE. HER ROOMMATES weren't there and she kept talking about "drama." I think these people sort of live in hell, fighting over scraps, over nothing. The house was disgusting. I offered to do the dishes after lunch and quickly went over the counters with some vinegar, I felt like maybe that was passive aggressive, but what can I do? Oothoon really does need my help if she's going to get out of this. She's 35 for God's sake, no one should be living like a slob at that age. But maybe that's the thing, I really did get a lot out of not being like her. I was a regular straight guy with a wife, maybe some kinks, and I've got money. So I could afford a little refinement.

That explains some of it, but I can't explain the way they tear each other down. Apparently everybody is abusing everybody else. I didn't follow the details. I felt a little instinctive solidarity with the bad ones and felt bad about that, but also I feel like this town must be full of people saying the exact same things about Oothoon and her friends? It's just a mess. I don't want people to hurt each other but I don't believe in this kind of back-biting either. "Calling out." And I think about people like Clive, where does he fit into all of this? Maybe there are some really scary ones, but it can't be that many. Whatever it is, I'm not scared of Oothoon or the bad girls, not even the really bad ones.

I went back out to the living room and she proceeded to natter on and on in this pushy way about how to transition. As if I'd asked. She was dropping these details into the conversation to make it tantalizing, as though I didn't know how. But I did my own research. I really did think it through, it just isn't me. It actually made me wonder if it was her either, like how insecure can you be, to have to recruit like this. I don't tell anybody to be a cuck. Besides, I know what people think about transwomen who transition in their forties. They say "if this was you all along, how come you didn't show us?" It wouldn't be the cool purple-hair universe for me. Besides, it isn't that cool! But here's Oothoon, desperate to convince me of something, or maybe to convince herself of something. I've got a show-me attitude about this stuff. Show me that you can be happy. Right now I don't see anything here to aspire to. Where's the Oothoon who swaggered up to us at the pool hall? Where's Oothoon the poet?

Paradoxically, I formed a kind of resolve there, I am going to pay for her surgery, and that's going to be my last word in the argument. I'm kind of convinced that she's staying in immaturity because her body is stuck in between like that. I told her that. I don't think she would have taken that from me, but I wrote her a check before I left. I think a lot of the funny gender politics and the fighting will go away when she gets what she needs. I don't have that need, so I think that means I'm not trans. I guess having a vagina would make things easier with Bill? I'm not even sure that it would. I want Oothoon to be a part of my world, instead of condescending to me and trying to get me to join her frankly miserable one. I feel like I'm in a haze of immaturity here. I have to get out.

Oothoon showed me more of her poems this time and I was surprised in a way by how bad they were. I don't know anything about poetry really, but I just mean she had sent me so deep into the library and is always talking about dead authors, but those people were a lot more serious about their craft. This is like punk rock with line breaks. There's so much rage at being trapped in this world and no effort at all to transcend it. Ok, Oothoon, your pain is real. I'm going to deliver you from it. I've never written a check for thirty thousand dollars before, but I think it's ok to do it once in my life. She deposited it on her phone while she was in the bathroom, I know because my bank called me with a fraud alert. No problem, I approved it. I'd be excited too.

RETURN

WHEN I ARRIVED HOME IN EUGENE I HAD A LOT OF TEXTS FROM Satori. Apparently Moonbeam got hurt at Tae Kwon Do? And one from Mindy saying we "need to talk." It all sounds very ominous. I need a shower. I was only gone for a few days, what the hell happened? More of that feeling of ascending the scaffold, that sick feeling in the stomach like I know I've fucked up. I started to remember that last conversation I'd had with Clive, about hurting Moonbeam. It can't be that, can it. I tried to comfort Satori, sending a lot of smileys. I think in some ways the infantilized style of Oothoon and her friends is rubbing off on me and taking some of the edge off of how I communicate. It's good, maybe. I shave my arms and I text like a teen girl, it just makes me a nice guy. A nice guy who takes out hits on his sexual rivals? I didn't ask for this. Apparently it's a spinal injury, likely to have some permanent consequences. Clive can't have known that, can he?

When I walked in the door, it felt like I was looking right through Mindy. I asked if she was feeling better after Clive and she said that she was, totally, but that it had had some consequences for her relationship with Kit. Apparently Kit's just sick of bi women, says they always finally prioritize men, and had given her an ultimatum. I don't know what it means. Is she going to leave me? Then she started asking me about money.

"I did write that check, yeah. We could talk about it."

"Well, did you check the balance first?" Mindy seemed distressed.

"Why would I—" we both paused. "Mindy, have you been dipping into my inheritance?" More silence. "How are we doing right now?"

Then she was in the other room. I'm still thinking about Satori. Am I poor now? Am I in debt? Could I reinvent myself as a working man? I imagined how it was at Bill's, with the guys, and I felt sick. I can't go down there, right down among em like that. Then I remembered the burger girl. Life finds a way, right? I think I'm going to vomit.

The world is so fucking evil, the only thing that made life possible was this little cushion. My wife, I've been betrayed by my wife. I looked in my wallet, 180 bucks and some change. I always take out 200 at the ATM and didn't end up spending as much as I thought in Reno. Am I going to have to stretch this out? I need a drink. I need some G. I need Clive's stupid enlightenment pills. I need to get fucked until there's nothing left. I don't know. I picked up the receiver and spun the dial for Bill. He asked if I was crying and I said no, an obvious lie. He said it was ok if I was and that I should come over.

"Ok, I'll bring beer."

"Don't be stupid, Darryl, I love you. Just come over." That shocked me, I don't think he'd said love before. I'd run to him but unfortunately it's three quarters of a mile and apparently I can only do half.

I just need to be in his arms for a little while. I can't figure this out right now. I can't do anything. My bags were still by the front door and I picked them up and started walking. No, this is stupid. Walked back two blocks, blew my nose and jumped in the car. That's what Bill would do.

But first I drove a long ways, out to Coburg, to the McKenzie river where I'd been a month ago with Patrick, just trying to pull myself together. What does it mean to pull myself back together? I don't want to pull myself together, I want to fall apart. I want Bill to see me. But he does see me. He said he loved me. He knew I was crying. He's been through so much with his brother, and the thought that Clive got away with it is just too much. I guess Clive's uncle had been a federal judge, and the cops all know him. They know not to fuck with him. They dropped the investigation, it never even went to court. He's above the law the way I'm above the economy. At least I thought I was. Now I'm a proletarian, but without the strength and solidity of those guys. Maybe the socialists can save me.

Unidentified number on my cellphone. "It's done." I hung up right away. That was Clive's voice. Why is he drawing me into this? I wonder if I can get out of here. Bill could come with me, he doesn't have a job right now. Breathe a little. Breathe. But breathing just makes me think about Moonbeam. Water in the river, the sunlight, he's in everything. Every moment I go in and out of this feeling, and it's going so fast. I could jump off this bridge but it's too low. Try. Think about Bill. He doesn't want to lose me. He's all I ever needed.

I glanced down the river and saw a stray dog again, the same one from the other day? Probably a bum's dog. Lately I see dogs everywhere. I don't know. It was night when I got back to the car. Where'd the time go? I put on the jazz station. You ever listen to Pharaoh Sanders? Kind of like a cross between John Coltrane and a beautiful goat from outer space. I felt ok for a second. Then I saw the cops and my heart rate went up. They're not looking for me, but my guilt is everywhere. I can't skip town right now. But I did skip town, I went to Reno. Clive knows that. He wants to implicate me. Jesus Christ, I meant a punch in the arm.

Spinal injuries are really bad, especially for a guy like Moonbeam. Everything about him, his concentrated smugness and spiritual air, is a bearing in his body. His body is disciplined and perfect, and so is his mind. What if he can't move right anymore, what if he has to take something for the pain, or get distracted by it, what if he can't fuck? It's like killing him. You can be disabled, I knew some people that are. But for Moonbeam that kills his whole world, it's like killing him, or worse than that. Clive has to know it. It wouldn't be the same kind of tragedy to fuck up my back, my body's nothing special, it isn't who I am. Clive has to know that.

Oothoon was obsessed with this piece by Tony Towle, which opens,

It was deduced in my mind quite early
that I would be spending time within its configurations,
and neglect somewhat
the more exhaustive aggrandizements of the body,
even as the natural victim in its whirlpool of references;
and now, perverse in an antidote for human loneliness,
I am reading Swinburne,
who confused these matters to a greater degree,
until he was constitutionally unfit for both,
passing gradually over the hot boundaries
and he has not been seen since.

Well, I don't know anything about Swinburne really, some kind British romantic? Favorite of TS Eliot? It's nothing deep. I don't know what the "hot boundaries" are. Why do we think we understand poetry? But this thing about refusing the body, yeah, I did that. Moonbeam didn't. He's an idiot in a way, but in his body he's a genius. Or he was. He isn't a brain, he's a spine. And Clive ruined his spine, and I asked, so it's like I did it.

What the hell was he thinking? Did he do this just so that someone could share his evil world? Is Moonbeam just material between us? It feels like when a cat makes gruesome work of a mouse or sparrow and brings it to you as some kind of gift. What kind of a gift is that, you little monster? Are you trying to prove to me that you're a killer? I already knew. How can I face Satori? Maybe I should avoid her.

Then I'm letting myself go into Pharaoh Sanders peaceful vibes, oceanic Moonbeam feelings. I'm going to listen to this show again, I've got to look it up, Thursday nights, late. And what the hell is Pharaoh Sanders talking about? "Greetings to Idris." I think that means something in Islam. I can never understand black music beyond a certain point, but this is so true. For a second I felt African. I felt human. I kept driving for a while and arrived at Bill's after midnight. He'd been worried about me, if it was drugs, if I'd run away, he said he called Mindy and she didn't pick up. He asked if I was alright and I said I was now, and ran to him with this beautiful sense of abandon. I didn't even shave, and I felt as he kissed me a kind of recoil from my stubble. I'm going to sneak off into the bathroom and shave and he won't know. I hope he can forget what that felt like.

I said "I'm sorry I'm a mess, I don't want to make you feel gay."

Bill sighed, and laughed a little, "We are gay, Darryl. I've been thinking about that. It must have been so hard for you not to push on that."

"I love you so much Bill. I feel like my life is ruined and it's all worth it for the chance to be with you. I could die right here in your arms." Was I really saying this? It felt like babble out of a romance novel.

"Darryl, no. It's not about dying, it's about living."

This is how Satori talks too. I love her too. I love her and I fucked it up. I can't fuck things up with Bill. Five minutes with Bill or Satori and life feels possible again. But they don't know how fucked up things are. I'm going to have to tell him.

PEPPER SPRAY

IN THE MORNING I TOLD BILL EVERYTHING, ABOUT THE MONEY, about Clive and Satori and Moonbeam. He looked sad and told me a little more about Brad. I guess I had never understood, Brad was dying, was depressed, and felt like being used by guys. He became kind of known in the fetish scene as a masochist who'd go further than anyone, but the meaning of it was sad. Like maybe if there'd been some kind of treatment he wouldn't have done that. Bill didn't go into what the illness was. I guess he'd died with Clive, who was going by Brian at the time, and a lot of people felt like that was a murder, others thought it was negligence. Satori's comments about Brad being a tourist started to make a little bit more sense to me, like Brad had used the BDSM community as a place to die, and everybody who makes that place home was left picking up the pieces. It's similar to people who commit suicide in a way, but different. I had a friend who did. I guess I almost did.

Bill for his part had always been a little torn up about whether he was gay. His little brother was gay. But Bill was just a complicated guy, he didn't want the identity, and he wasn't femi-nine. And then gay became this place where Brad had gotten hurt. I guess you never know what people are going through. If Bill can be gay do I still have to be feminine? Whatever, I'm not doing it for him. I'm not doing it to be trans either. All I want to be is smooth and slight and the little spoon. I'm not going to take hormones. I'm fucked up enough as it is.

He said it was probably better for me not to talk about it with Satori if I thought I couldn't lie about it but that if I lied to her even once, the relationship I have with her would never be the same. When did Bill get so deep? That's exactly right. It'd be ok if she never asked, maybe, but what if she asks? He said I should lay low for a while and asked after a pause if I knew how to use a gun. Before I could answer he handed me a pepper spray keychain and told me to wear my running shoes everywhere.

No problem, but I ran the other day and had to catch my breath in just half a mile. I felt the belly feeling again and looked up at him. I didn't have to say anything. "Jump in the shower," he grinned. Then I don't know, I was clean and face down on the bed and he was fucking me so hard I thought I'd die. I was crying, saying "thank you" over and over again and my voice was so gentle, it wasn't put on. This is all I need. Why do I have to go clean up the mess I've made of my life, I just want to stay here. I don't know.

After a long moment I asked Bill if we could run away to Reno. Oothoon owes me a big favor, she'd help us hide. He didn't say anything and I realized he was asleep. I'm kind of glad he didn't hear the suggestion. In the morning I crept out of the room without waking him up and put my clothes on, still feeling the weight of him inside me, like I'd been turned into a new person. Surgery can't compare, what the hell is Oothoon thinking.

THE ABSOLUTE MASTER

EVERYTHING IS FINE, IN A WAY. I'VE BEEN LIVING WITH BILL FOR the last couple weeks out of my little bag, still haven't gone back to the house. The way Bill lives, it's ok. Spartan. Takes me back to when I was in college, living off campus for a year and not quite knowing how to live. I'm a lot better at it now: I do the dishes, I cook better breakfasts. What I ought to do is check in on Mindy but I'm still mad about the money. I'm sure she is too. I just have no idea what's going on there. I don't know if I even care anymore. I had the thought that if it burns down, I could collect the insurance money and walk away. But I don't need more scandal in my life. That's what Clive would do. I know what that leads to.

I met Satori and Moonbeam for coffee and he said he's starting to feel better, that he's gotten off of the oxycontin and takes a lot of weed tincture. I can see the pain in his eyes and he doesn't feel as clear or as powerful. I went in for a hug and he recoiled a little, he seemed scared of me. Maybe just protecting his back. Or am I seeing things? Is that my guilt? I remember the feeling of him almost seeming to control my mind. Maybe he can see what I'm thinking now. I don't think he can, he's too high. I asked him if he expected a full recovery and Satori cut me off very sharply. I guess it's a rude question. So I played it cool, and I asked how it had happened.

"There's this asshole I do Tae Kwon Do with, named Clive or Brian or something."

I just said, "Oh, no."

"I almost feel like it was intentional. We're both black belts, 4 dan." Ok, Moonbeam. "At our level sparring is about control. I could kill him, he could kill me, I guess he almost did. But that's not what it's about, it's supposed to feel like a dance."

I think this was the most coherent thought I'd ever heard from Moonbeam, I guess now that he hasn't got a spine he has to be a brain. I felt a little inner smile as I said, "I guess I wouldn't know, but yeah, that's fucked up."

"Darryl, have you talked to Clive? Satori says you're both friends with him. I don't get that, Darryl. You act like you're scared of me. But you hang out with Clive? I need to know what's going on. When I'm put back together I need to have a conversation with him, and maybe with you too." Moonbeam, continuing to be coherent and reasonable, will wonders never cease?

"I haven't talked to him in a month or two." The first lie, I thought. And suddenly I could see Clive, in a scene in February, saying that he would "make me know the fear of death, the absolute master." It sounded very biblical. Is this what he meant? I felt very cold and like him for a second, it was like the air had gone out of the room.

"Darryl, are you carrying pepper spray?" Satori cocked her head sideways looking at the thing on my keychain.

"Yeah, I mean, you never know, right?" I keep playing things cool.

"Never know about what?" Satori was pressing me.

"There were a few robberies recently down the block from me. Tweakers. I don't know, it's hard to talk about."

"Ok Darryl, but I don't like violent energy in my space. Can you not bring that thing back here again? I've never seen you carry it before."

"Absolutely, um. I'm sorry for not asking you. I'll leave it in the car next time." So I've just gotta make it from the car to the door.

DAMN COFFEE 2

For a week since having tea with Satori and Moonbeam and she hasn't been returning my texts, and I was starting to get that sick panic feeling again. Then I got one reply: "You make me fucking sick, Darryl. I know about you and Clive. You can't even be real enough to apologize? You'd better not show your face around me, Moonbeam, or Patrick EVER again. DON'T reply to this."

Of course I replied. Of course we talked on the phone. She said that she loved me and that I'd betrayed her, and that she couldn't trust me to be around anymore, and that was non-negotiable. She said she was never planning to leave me for Moonbeam, that it was just a nice, light connection, and that he actually annoyed her a little in the same way I was annoyed with him. But they'd gotten a little closer as she was helping him get back to health this week. She said that there was a lot of hate in me, which I think might be right, mostly for myself. But it spills over and I hurt people. I guess that's true too. She said I don't seem to care about Mindy, and that maybe Mindy is just trying to get me to notice her. Even Bill says that, he says everything I want is tied up with death. But he has time for me, he's always pushing me to go deeper with my feelings. And well, so was Satori until I put a hit on her boyfriend.

I don't know what I can do, you know. I thought I was going

to lose Satori to Moonbeam, but I didn't think it would be like this, that it would be my fault, that I'd have fucked everything up. At least it doesn't sound like they want to press charges. They know about Clive, they know how he is. Nobody wants to make a move. So maybe we're ok. But I want to make a move. And nobody knows what Clive will do next. I've been trying to ignore the calls I get, from blocked numbers and payphones. Is he hoping I'll thank him?

I had a wife, I had a girlfriend. Where the hell am I now. This afternoon I finally picked up the phone. Of course it was Clive, in that cold voice "I'm glad you've agreed to talk. Would you meet me at the Starbucks?" Always fucking Starbucks. He's a killer without taste. I said I would. "Ten minutes." Why not. I wanted to do this before Bill got home. I grabbed my pepper spray and strolled out the door. In seconds, Clive was walking alongside me.

"How did you know I was here?"

"I know all kinds of things, Darryl. I've been here before."

"Brad?"

"Careful, Darryl. Don't say that name."

Fingering my carabiner I noticed that Clive had somehow removed my pepper spray from the chain. Sleight of hand. So much for that. We walked the rest of the way to Starbucks in silence. I followed his lead and ordered a decaf Americano— 175 bucks left—, then we sat face to face in the generic half-retro space that could have been in Reno or Eugene or fucking anywhere.

"Did you like what I did?"

"No!"

Clive was smiling. "I did it because you asked me to, Darryl. You should thank me."

I tried to explain that I didn't mean it like that, it was all too far, I meant a punch in the arm. Something humbling, but not permanent.

"You should have said. And anyway, isn't he humbled? Don't you like him better now?"

"Clive, did you talk to Satori?"

"Of course."

"Did you tell her that I asked you to do it?"

"I told her exactly what you said. You said, 'Make it hurt.'"

"I could turn you in, Clive."

"For what, exactly? I think you ought to begin to show a little more gratitude. As your therapist—" Clive snickered a little and I reflected that this might have been the first time I'd heard him laugh.

"Fuck you Clive! Just let me live. I can't feel this guilty anymore!"

Funny looks from the staff, I'd raised my voice, I was shouting. Clive suggested that we take a walk. How could I refuse him now? Clive is in control.

DRIVE

A LONG DRIVE IN CLIVE'S CAR, WITH MORE JAZZ ON THE RADIO BUT nothing like the other night, something fusion-y and mean, like Miles Davis on cocaine. And of course it really is Miles Davis on cocaine, it's "On the Corner." I can't believe I'm still asking about the music. But it feels so matter of fact. I'm going to die. After a few minutes I stopped answering his questions. "It doesn't really matter what I say now, does it, Clive?" Clive nodded and kept driving. I noticed a little blue water bottle.

"GHB?"

"Yeah," and he hands me a flask. "Drink."

I could use it as a weapon maybe, while it's full. But it's useless to fight anymore. So I just ask, "Clive, where are we going?" Little sip.

"Mount Pisgah, like we planned."

So we're taking that hike. Was this part of the plan too? We spent the rest of the drive in silence and sharp trumpet lines that all go wrong and it's all too fast, watching impossible buckets of rain hit the windshield and slide nowhere. And with Miles still mocking me, we were in the arboretum, side by side in silence up the trail, blue bottle slightly poking out of Clive's low-fashion fanny pack and absurd white basketball shoes, now soaking wet. The fact that he has no style kills me. He has no anything.

I couldn't believe I was thinking about fashion but I was, just like the music. Wasn't I supposed to have clarity? Wasn't I supposed to see my life flash before my eyes? Instead it's a blue gatorade bottle with the label peeled off and the most evil electric jazz ever. Am I already in hell? I remember when I first met Clive I thought of him like Hannibal Lecter but Lecter was cultured, that's the joke of him, this guy is nothing. Just a void that doesn't want to be seen. But that's it maybe. Being seen. He has to control how others see him, and that's where I fucked up. I thought I'd try.

"Clive, you don't have to be scared. I see you, I know you, and I don't hate you."

Clive's eyes tightened a bit. "You'll change your mind, like they all do. You won't forget what you know, and you'll tell the others. You've shown me that your conscience is a liability. Now stop fighting me."

"Clive, you don't have to do this. We could both walk away." But the words sounded weak in my mouth, like I didn't even believe them myself. Maybe Clive is the predator, I'm the prey, it's as simple as that. I'm another Brad. Like arguing with an owl. There's no way I can prevail on his compassion, because there is none, and no way I can prevail on his reason, which is always a thousand steps ahead of mine. He held out his hand. "Phone." His voice has this hypnotic absoluteness, there was no question of resisting. I handed him my phone. He nimbly removed the battery and handed it back to me. Then he made an unfamiliar sound, as if he were calling a bird and looked around. Is he really not human?

Whatever sense he had told him something was clearly the matter, and we sped up, panting and covered in mud by the time we reached the top. So much for his new shoes. The rain had given way and everything was bright.

Lately I feel like I'm ascending the scaffold all the time, except when I actually am, and then I feel bright and alive and in nature. Go figure. It reminded me of how Moses doesn't enter the promised land, he just gets one glimpse of it from a mountaintop and dies. God let him see. Where's my glimpse?

I gestured to the bottle, "Are you going to make me drink that stuff?"

"Yes, Darryl. I am."

I started to think about it, back in January I'd overdosed on the same stuff. He even used the same blue food coloring I'd always used with mine. He's got it, down to the sweetener. Everybody thought it was a suicide then, so for sure they'd think it now. My hand went to my left pocket, to my phone, not even for help, just for the familiar weight of it in my hand. Too light. Right, no battery. I was breathing fast and Clive sat me beneath a tree to get out of the rain. A small mercy.

It was sun-showering now and all I could think about was the drops of water on the waxy leaves, Moonbeam again. A leaf broken off. Clive suggested that I begin "composing my thoughts," which surprised me. I thought he'd have a fake suicide note already written. I said I wouldn't do that for him. "That's fine," he said. "That's fine, I was just giving you a chance if you had something to say. Maybe you wanted to say goodbye to Bill." He paused, "or anybody else."

Do I really have nothing to say? I was staring at the sun, my soul seeming to want to fall in. Bill, Satori, am I dead already? I can let go right now, that's actually easier than hanging on another moment to say goodbye. Then chaos. A shot rings out, and for a moment we're suspended in the abyss of the click. Time stops and then starts again, and Clive is on the ground, clutching his leg, with Bill standing over him.

Bill, my love. My savior. My bull. We walked together very quietly down the hill. There was nothing to say about what he'd done for me.

I don't know if Clive can die. But I know he wasn't dead. I asked Bill if we should call the police and he shook his head. If we should bury him, make sure he's dead. Again no. No one knows we're here. We can get away. And I think I know the way. But is Reno far enough?

"Where'd you get the motorcycle, Bill?"

"From Patrick, he won't miss it. Hop on. And hold on tight."

I started to say something but it was lost in the rain and the roar.

—*Eugene, New York, Portland, Philadelphia, Halifax 2016-2020*

ACKNOWLEDGMENTS

Battling a tendency to name everyone I've ever known here, I'll list just a few of the people who made this project possible since its advent in 2016, in a flash with Amy's photo. Some helped with the text, some with advice, and some lived their advice. In the text as in life, any infelicities are mine and no endorsement is implied.

Thanks to Zoë B, Jae Bearhat, Isobel Bess, Imogen Binnie, J Birdhead, Cliff Cannon, Abassi Dubiaku, George Dust, Cat Fitzpatrick, Lucca Fraser, Kay Gabriel, Peli Grietzer, Stephen Ira, Frog K, Lindsay Lerman, Rachel Blum Levy, Kevin Lin, Kyle Lukoff, K, The Gray Man, Amy Marvin, Momus, Elle Mundy, Geoffrey H Nicholson, Brian Ng, Never Angeline Nørth, Rosary O, Zach Ozma, Krissy Page, Torrey Peters, Sridhar Ramesh, RMB, Adrian Rome, Sarah Schulman, Julian Shendelman, Belacqua Shuah, Clem Snide, Violet Spurlock, Captain Strobe Lou Sullivan, T, Eero Talo, M. Teste, Athena Thiessen, Jeanne Thornton, McKenzie Wark, and so many more.

Thanks as well to the participants of the Bay Area Trans Writers Workshop, the 2016 Topside Summer Writing Workshop, to the Boys in the Band, the Fifths, and the Six.

And thanks of course to Leza Cantoral and Christoph Paul at CLASH Books.

Jackie Ess
Halifax
September 2020

ABOUT THE AUTHOR

Photo of trees at Skinner Butte, Eugene, OR taken by Amy Marvin, December 2016"

Jackie Ess is a writer, cultural mischief-maker, and minor internet celebrity, as we all are now. A co-founder of the Bay Area Trans Writers Workshop, her work can be found in Heavy Feather Review, the Zahir, the New Inquiry, Vetch, and the anthology *We Want It All: An Anthology of Radical Trans Poetics*. *Darryl* is her first novel. Find her on Twitter @jackie_ess.

ALSO BY CLASH BOOKS

MARGINALIA

Juno Morrow

GIRL IN THE WALLS

Katy Michelle Quinn

BORN TO BE PUBLIC

Greg Mania

LIFE OF THE PARTY

Tea Hacic

HEXIS

Charlene Elsby

GIRL LIKE A BOMB

Autumn Christian

I'M FROM NOWHERE

Lindsay Lerman

COMAVILLE

Kevin Bigley

SILVERFISH

Rone Shavers

POINTS OF ATTACK

Mark de Silva

WE PUT THE LIT IN LITERARY

clashbooks.com

FOLLOW US

Twitter

IG

FB

@clashbooks

EMAIL

clashmediabooks@gmail.com

PUBLICITY

McKenna Freiss

clashbookspublicity@gmail.com

Printed in the USA
CPSIA information can be obtained
at www.ICGtesting.com
JSHW022341140824
68134JS00019B/1611

9 781944 866846